SIOUX FALLS PUBLIC LIBRARY
Sioux Falls, SD

User Information

Borrowing Material

You are held responsible for all material borrowed using the borrower's card issued to you. You must have this card with you to borrow materials.

Length of Loan

A date due slip is provided when you borrow items.

> **If you have questions about when an item is due, please call.**

Fines

A fine will be charged for damaged, overdue, or lost materials.

Care of Materials

Please do not mend items at home.

Please carry items in protective bags when the weather is bad. Please do not keep plastic media in overheated cars.

Library and Bookmobile Schedules

Please ask for a schedule. The Library is closed on legal holidays.

Please return!
Others are waiting!

WESTERN
PERFORMANCE

Also by Tommie Kirksmith

RIDE WESTERN STYLE:

A GUIDE FOR YOUNG RIDERS

WESTERN PERFORMANCE

A GUIDE FOR
YOUNG RIDERS

Tommie Kirksmith

HOWELL BOOK HOUSE
New York

MAXWELL MACMILLAN CANADA
Toronto

MAXWELL MACMILLAN INTERNATIONAL
New York   Oxford   Singapore   Sydney

Howell Book House
Macmillan Publishing Company
866 Third Avenue
New York, NY 10022

Maxwell Macmillan Canada, Inc.
1200 Eglinton Avenue East
Suite 200
Don Mills, Ontario M3C 3N1

Macmillan Publishing Company is part
of the Maxwell Communication Group of Companies.

Library of Congress Cataloging-in-Publication Data
Kirksmith, Tommie.
    Western performance : a guide for young riders / Tommie Kirksmith.
        p.   cm.
    Includes index.
    ISBN 0-87605-844-6
    1. Horse-shows—Western divisions and classes.   2. Western show
horses.   I. Title.
SF296.W47K57   1992
798.2—dc20   92-11264   CIP

This book is not intended as a substitute for professional advice and
guidance in the field of horseback riding. A young person should take
part in the activities discussed in this book only under the supervision
of a knowledgeable adult.

Macmillan books are available at special discounts for bulk
purchases for sales promotions, premiums, fund-raising, or
educational use. For details, contact:

Special Sales Director
Macmillan Publishing Company
866 Third Avenue
New York, NY 10022

10 9 8 7 6 5 4 3 2 1

Printed in the United States of America

CONTENTS

FOREWORD

------◆►◄◆------

"Knowledge gained should be knowledge shared." "That which is learned should be passed on to be used over and again." "Without knowledge, we can't progress." These and similar adages have been an integral part of my philosophy as long as I can remember.

Being a firm believer in the power of the printed word and the need for quality equine books, I feel Tommie Kirksmith has done an excellent job in describing, via a commonsense approach, the way a rider and horse should work together. She grooms a rider to think by being prepared to act or react when necessary and to better understand his or her particular horse—its strong points, abilities and weaknesses, and how to use each to the rider's advantage.

Every chapter offers an abundance of information about a particular subject, but throughout the book a thread is woven. Enjoy your horses for what they are and not for what you can force them to be against their nature. Your horse will tell you everything, if you care to listen. The examples of how to prepare, analyze and show, together with observing how the judge reacts to you, are quite informative. Thinking in harmony with your horse is a basic for beginner and professional alike.

Whether you've just gotten into the horse world or have been around awhile, there are always clues to make you think and hopefully become a better horseman. Many clues remain constant through the years, and this book teaches you how to spot them. For instance, "think soft and prepare the mind" is underlying throughout. Tommie describes, in understandable terms, how the horse works and how to work with the horse. There is a time to work and a time to relax, which may be individual to each horse, as every horse is different, and so is every rider. Some learn rapidly, others more slowly; personalities and dispositions are diverse, and working together is the only way.

Planning ahead is stressed, along with being able to think like a horse. A horse's mind can absorb just so much, and Tommie teaches you methods of determining what to do to keep 'em comfortable, keep 'em happy and eager for the next lesson. These are the basics, and Tommie has demonstrated a complete understanding of unity.

Getting into the real world of showing is well defined. Horse shows have changed over the years and will continue to do so. However, the basics of working with your horse will never change, and this goes along with the quality of life with horses and the intimacy of experiences shared. This book is a must for every "horsehold."

DON BURT

ACKNOWLEDGMENTS

First I'll thank two persons I've never met (not at the time of writing this, anyway) who deserve credit for their clarification of some important points in this book.

Deb Bennett, Ph.D., a natural history researcher with the Smithsonian Institution, specializes in horses. She has a rare ability to simplify complicated structural details about horses (and riders) and make them fun to learn. Thanks for your help, Dr. Deb!

Performance Horseman magazine published a series of articles on Penny Gibbs's system for preparing a trail horse. I introduced Penny's methods to Dual Cutlass (Spock), my big Paint who'd spent most of his twenty years performing dressage and jumping (English), working a few cattle (Western) and being a South Texas beach bum (bareback). Even at his advanced age, Spock had no problem learning Penny's signals.

Gene Brown, the photographer of *Ride Western Style*, my first book, also took the photos for this book. Believe me, it wasn't easy. We had to slip our picture-taking sessions in between thunderstorms and our models leaving town for horse shows.

Terry McCutcheon heads the Equine Program for Cooke County College in Gainesville, Texas. He let us use the college facilities and, in general, helped us get pictures. He read this book in manuscript and added some points to what I'd said about roping, which is Terry's rodeo specialty.

Champion reiner Craig Johnson and his wife, Lynn, taught their daughter how to ride. From the looks of things, another champion Johnson is on her way. We took pictures of eight-year-old Sarah performing reining moves on her Quarter Horse, Going Formal (Arizona)—and some special moves involving her pony, Misty—at their Gainesville ranch.

Bo Smith, fourteen, lives with his parents on their horse farm in Valley View, Texas. Bo adds variety to our pictures dominated by Quarter Horses. Besides his other accomplishments, Bo earned a 4-H Youth Superior Championship on his Tennessee Walking Horse mare, Delight of Jet Star. Bo's mother, Bonnie, is responsible for home-grown Delight's early schooling. Then Bo took over and the real fun began.

The picture of Kylie Barrick, eleven, winning the Josey Barrel Racing Clinic Spring Competition appeared in our local newspaper. I remembered Kylie taking barrel racing lessons from my friend Shirley Robben. When I called Kylie's parents (Marilyn and Keith Barrick) and asked if Kylie could be our barrel racing model for this book, I learned that her fourteen-year-old brother Ty is involved in roping. I needed a roper model, too. After getting pictures of roping equipment and some things involving the roping horse, I next asked Ty to rope a calf and tie it. Ty agreed. I didn't know until afterward that Ty had roped many a calf, then thrown and tied calves that were staked to a fence. But he had never put all the pieces together. Photos of Ty's first complete calf-roping are permanently recorded in this book. (Too bad we couldn't include sound effects of his struggle!)

Kyle Manion, Teresa Padgett and Sunny Gayden were in *Ride Western Style*. Kyle rode in the prestigious American Quarter Horse Congress pleasure classes as a little guy. Now fifteen, he works for his dad (noted trainer/rider Tommy Manion) and competes quite successfully with his Quarter cutting horse gelding, Smooth Eliminator. Teresa (also fifteen) trains her own horses for both Western and English performance. Her AQHA and 4-H winnings would take at least a full page to list, so I won't. Sunny, fifteen, is presently interested in other activities and doesn't take her Roosterama around the barrels very often. Those great pictures of Sunny "bailing out" that were in *Ride Western Style* appear in this book also.

Most of the pictures of Teresa were taken at her place, but the cutting horse pictures were made at the Jones Ranch. If you remember the Vestal children, Cyrus and Erin, from *Ride Western Style*, you'll recognize them in the background helping with the cattle.

INTRODUCTION

If you read my first book, *Ride Western Style*, you'll recognize Primo. That's what we call your horse. If you haven't already read about Primo and his ways, you may have to work harder now at learning to think like a horse. (By the way, if you plan to control Primo by brute force rather than by reaching his mind, you're reading the wrong guide.)

Western Performance carries Western riding beyond the novice level. It's written for the young rider who wants to show or work the Western performance horse. Primo should be a well-broke horse. You're not quite ready for a green colt. And you don't need a horse that, for whatever reason (lack of talent, spoiled, goes lame, too old), you can't compete on.

This book teaches you the kind of control that keeps Primo listening to you. If he's a push-button pony that does everything automatically, two things are almost certain to happen. First, you won't be able to ride any horse for this activity except Primo. Second, you won't be able to correct Primo when, sooner or later, he realizes he can do whatever he pleases with you as his rider. You want Primo to be well trained. In the real world, however, even a champion performer needs regular practice and some fine tuning.

Western riding is a big beautiful picture puzzle made from lots of little pieces. Some pieces are more important for your particular picture puzzle than other pieces. I can't say, without knowing you and your plans, what advice you need to get the most out of your horse. That's why I urge you to read and study every chapter in this book, not just the parts about your favorite kind of riding. You might find a helpful piece of roping information in the chapter on trail class. Or you might find the answer to your problem with barrel racing in the chapter on equitation or the one on reining.

I've tried to shed light on practically every type of Western performance, including showing at halter. But I've concentrated more on Western pleasure, equitation, trail and timed speed events (barrel racing and such). Because I don't have lots of cutting and roping experience, I asked very capable cutters and ropers (of varied ages) who live nearby for their expert help with the parts of this that deal with those topics.

CHAPTER 1

General Information About Primo

What Is a Western Performance Horse?

A performance horse is more than a saddle horse ridden purely for pleasure. This horse is highly trained and conditioned to respond to his rider's signals. The rider need not be distracted by arguing with his horse. Whatever goal the rider has, whether he's riding Western or English style, he depends on his performance horse as a teammate.

Generally we think of a Western performance horse as being the best horse to ride while performing cowboy-type activities. He works under a stock-seat saddle and is steered by looser reins than a horse ridden English style.

More American Quarter Horses are used for Western performance activities than any other breed, followed by Paints, Appaloosas, Arabians and Morgans. However, this doesn't mean that a horse of another breed or type can't be just as capable, for example, Half-Quarter, Half-Arab, Tennessee Walker, Mustang and unregistered (grade) horses.

Every rule has some exceptions, but it's sensible to fit a horse's build and temperament to the activity he's asked to perform. Western performance activities combine quick moves and tight patterns with relaxed, easy gaits. The horse is often asked to go from one extreme to the other. Logically, this should be easier for a more compact, easygoing horse to handle than for a horse with longer legs and a built-in urge to run.

Some Western performance horses are called *stock horses* because they're trained to control "stock," which is short for "livestock." (In Chapter 6 you'll learn another meaning for stock horse.) Although horses, sheep and goats are livestock, the word is mainly used to refer to cattle. The stock horse has been the cowboy's valued partner ever since the American cowboy was "invented" (around 1820). The stock horse must be able to perform a variety of tasks in a constantly changing order. He never knows if he'll spend the day standing around while his rider mends fences or if he'll have to carry his rider through some hard gallops and fast turns. He was, until recently, trained a little differently in Texas than in California and everywhere else. The main difference had to do with how his rider used the reins. Texas-style training called for looser contact.

Today's working stock horse has the same duties as his ancestors. He helps round up and move stock that have spread out to graze many acres of land. Then he helps when an animal needs to be separated from the rest of the herd for individual attention.

You can still find a real working stock horse and his cowboy partner. But there aren't as many now as in former years. Land is too valuable as real estate to be used for grazing. Open ranges are being taken over by growing cities. Today's stock horse will more likely be found in a show or rodeo arena. He'll work to help round up prizes instead of a scattered herd.

If the stock horse moves, separates and holds a herd of cattle, he's a *cutting horse*. A *roping horse* moves into a position that enables his rider to get a rope on a calf (or maybe a full-sized steer). Then he backs up and keeps just enough pressure on the rope to hold the noose without pulling the calf off its feet while his rider dismounts and ties the calf. Sometimes he moves in so his rider can transfer from the saddle onto a steer and wrestle it down. A *pick-up horse* moves into position so his rider can help another rider get off a bucking horse or bull. The stock horse was originally asked to do these things, and more, working on the ranch.

Some Western performance horses are reining horses. Like the stock horse, a good *reining horse* is quick, strong and flexible. However, the stock horse is trained to respond to the cattle in addition to his rider, but the reining horse specializes in obeying his rider. For reining and Western riding events, this horse moves at different gaits and in several definite patterns. A working cow horse does both cutting and reining routines.

There's a lot of fast action in the performance activities that have been described so far. A horse trained for trail class usually moves slower. The *trail horse* is a special kind of reining horse. This mannerly horse goes sideways, backward and forward with precision accuracy. In class he carefully works his way over or around obstacles, proving his obedience to his rider and his handiness for trail rides and ranch errands. Using those guidelines, you could consider the pick-up horse used in rodeos as a specialized trail horse.

The performance horse can also be a *speed horse*. A *racehorse* tries to outrun other horses who compete with him on a mostly straight course. We don't emphasize that kind of speed in this book. However, we do discuss Western timed speed events, the most popular event being barrel racing.

Long-distance rides (endurance racing, competitive trail riding, Ride and Tie) are becoming more popular. They compare with the Pony Express, or perhaps the long-distance rides of the U.S. Cavalry before World War II. Any style of saddle is permitted, but most riders choose a stock-seat saddle for its comfort and security. Horse and rider cover 25 to 100 miles, usually over rough country, as fast as possible. Before, during and after the race, the horse's physical condition is checked. Vets check his vital signs (pulse, breathing and such) and look for possible lameness. All the horses are expected to grow tired during the race, but those that recover more quickly during required rests get better scores. For most competitions, that score counts as much as the horse/rider's order of finish. If you're interested in long-distance riding activities, see Appendix 3 for further information.

Why Primo Should Be a Finished Horse

To say that Primo is *finished* doesn't mean he's over the hill and no longer much fun to ride. A finished horse has been broken to ride and trained to obey his rider's signals. He's well-broke.

The opposite of finished is *green*. A green horse is barely broke and has no idea of what he's expected to do. The horse operates by instincts at first. Then he learns by some repetition, some reward and punishment and some "monkey see, monkey do" with other horses. A good trainer teaches everything in terms that the horse can understand. He thinks like a horse. To be a good rider, so should you.

It's not unusual for a green horse to become easily frightened and forget all about his rider. He may even buck and act like he thinks the rider is a hungry mountain lion on his back.

Riding an animal that weighs at least a thousand pounds and is out of control is no one's idea of fun. That's one reason why you should leave green or spoiled horses to experienced trainers.

Why a Green Rider Shouldn't Ride a Performance Horse

There's more to racing around barrels, reining a pattern, handling trail obstacles and facing a cow than meets the eye. If your goal is to ride a Western performance horse, learn your riding fundamentals on a finished Western riding (saddle) horse. Have your first experience with as many different situations as possible while riding a calm horse. This is the best way to keep riding a safe and enjoyable experience.

Your balance and basic control of the horse should be very good before you trade Old Faithful for a horse that is trained to react to your moves in a more competitive way. A performance horse can make some special moves that are faster and/or more advanced than those ordinary riding horses make.

A typical performance horse is more sensitive to cues than a typical pleasure horse. He'll respond more quickly than you may be ready for. Let's pretend you say "Whoa!" if you want to slow him down. "Whoa" should only mean "stop," not "slow down." Even Old Faithful should stop for "Whoa." But this performance horse stops so quickly that you could lose balance and fall off. By the way, we call Old Faithful a pleasure horse. Generally, however, Old Faithful would need a lot of fine tuning (meaning an improved way of responding to your signals) to win at Western Pleasure.

Let's say you don't fall off, but you're still out of balance. So you pull on the rein and shift in the saddle to regain your balance. Your horse might mistake the tightened rein and shift in weight as signals for a spin or a rollback. Now this could really get you into trouble!

Whether he slams on the brakes or turns out from under you, the horse would only be doing what he was trained to do. These are just two examples. The possibilities are endless. Then, and we're still pretending, let's say that you disciplined the horse for "not obeying."

How would *you* feel about being punished for doing as you were taught? Well, he wouldn't like it either. By the time you learned what your rein cue and shifted weight really meant to your trained performance horse, he wouldn't respond in the same way he'd been taught.

If he's the type that wants to please his rider and avoid trouble, he would ignore that signal. After receiving it a couple of times, this polite performance horse would do as Old Faithful did when you were learning to ride. If you kept kicking or yanking the rein, Old Faithful learned to ignore those signals. He "tuned you out."

Likewise, and we're not pretending now, a more laid-back performance horse will discover that he can get away with being sloppy. He'll get lazy and find an easier way to do things. He'll never do anything dangerous on purpose. He just won't do the job he was trained to do until he's convinced by some really good riding to do it again.

A highly trained performance horse who's also high strung often becomes confused or annoyed by incorrect signals. He'll react to a rider's mistakes by misbehaving. After this happens a couple of times, he can become spoiled. A good trainer can straighten him out; however, once a spoiled horse has been retrained, he should be ridden only by good riders or under expert supervision. Otherwise he can cause trouble again. One little mistake could make him either blow up or give up. Such a horse is unpredictable as a performer and maybe even dangerous.

You'd probably be safe with the laid-back performance horse I described. He would be ideal for you to ride while learning performance activities. In fact, let's call this one Primo.

How This Book Can Help You with Primo

No matter how great Primo is or how good a rider you are, you need each other. The better you understand what he is supposed to do, the better you'll both perform.

That's what this book is for. It's to help teach you how to ride and show a Western performance horse. You might be able to study this book on your own and use what you learn from it to win at shows or to work cattle. That's possible. There is no limit to what you and Primo can do as a team. Nevertheless, a good coach would make it easier for you to reach your full potential on Primo. After you've read this book (and *Ride Western Style*), you might want to combine what you've learned here with what a coach could offer while watching you ride Primo.

Further Help with Your Riding

I would like to mention four items that can do a lot to improve your riding.

The first is a camcorder—an updated movie camera. Low prices and simplified operations have made this gadget almost as popular as the video cassette recorder (VCR). If you do get a camcorder, you'll need someone to operate it. That person should understand Western riding, in order to know what to shoot and so you won't have to shout instructions while you ride. If a camcorder is too expensive for your family, there are several options. You can rent one. You can borrow one. Or you can share the expenses of a camcorder with other riders you know and like. This last option may be even better than owning your own camcorder.

The second is a VCR. You'll need one in order to watch videos of yourself and Primo. I can think of no better way to learn what you're doing (right or wrong) than to study videos of your riding. Snapshots are nice, but they can't show the whole story. You need a VCR with controls that allow you to slow the motion or even stop on one picture. If you can slow the video's motion, you'll see details of action that happen too fast for the eye to follow and "explain" to the brain.

The third is a good instructional video. A wide variety of performance training videos are available, and instead of buying them you can borrow or rent them.

My fourth suggestion is to build, borrow or buy a set of dressage letters for your arena (or corner of the pasture or wherever). Dressage letters are placed around an area and down a center line, as shown in the diagram. They'll help you mark off spots for almost any kind of riding pattern.

Help from the Experts

Most of the magazine articles written by trainers, riders, judges, vets, farriers or other equine specialists can help you. Most books and videos by professionals can be very helpful also.

The videos are especially meaningful after you've read and ridden enough to have increased your knowledge and developed a feel so you'll know what to look for. You can learn as much from what you *see* as from what the video narrator says. Maybe you'll see how to do something that you've had trouble with, but it's not even mentioned by the narrator (who's often the rider). This is because the video is about something else. In this case, you get a bonus.

Sometimes, however, the narrator will "explain" what he's getting the horse to do. Yet you'll plainly see the horse do something quite different from what this person says he's doing. Seeing is believing, right? Most of the time, yes. But you might have misunderstood something the narrator said or that you saw because you don't see it from the same angle he does.

Occasionally you can get incorrect information from magazine articles. Here's why:

- The writer doing the interviewing is no expert. So he failed to report a vital fact included but not emphasized in the interview with the expert. He didn't realize the information's importance and left it out because it didn't sound right to him, or it made the article too long. Maybe he tried to report accurately, but lack of familiarity with the subject caused him to get a few steps in the wrong order or use a word incorrectly.
- Maybe the writer got everything right, but then the editor at the magazine changed something because it didn't sound right or dropped paragraphs that made the article too long.

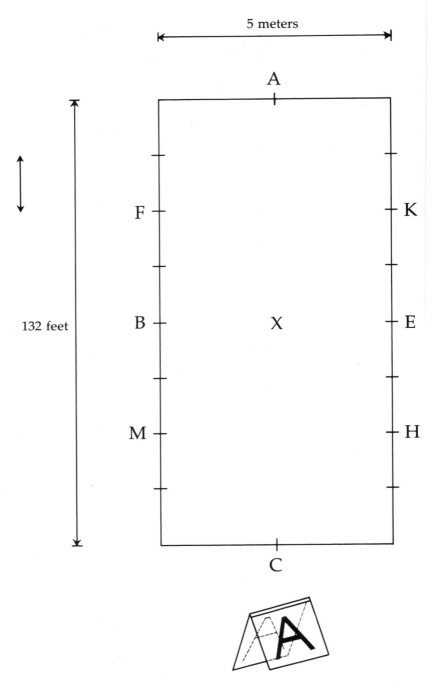

5 meters

A

132 feet

F   K

B   X   E

M   H

C

letter model (showing both sides)

- Often several different people will work on an article before you read it in a magazine. Sometimes pictures and drawings, or the captions under them, get switched around or mixed up with material from another article.
- Maybe the expert only describes the ideal situation with the perfect horse or the perfect rider. He doesn't mention problems that can happen to anybody.
- Occasionally there's a winning rider or trainer who works mainly by instinct. He can't really tell you why or how he gets the horse to do so well. So, when he's asked to explain his secrets, he may be unwilling to share them, or he may come up with something that's not really what he does.

This is to say, take what you read with a grain of salt. In the case of magazine articles, readers often find the mistakes and write in to the editor. Such letters are later published in the Letters to the Editor section of the magazine.

You don't need to question everything you read. Use good judgment, though, and perhaps talk to a knowledgeable horse person. Don't be too quick to change your old ways and try something new just because it's in a magazine. Because it worked for last year's world champion doesn't mean

Dressage Letters

The letters A, K, E, H, C, M, B, F and X are arranged as shown in the illustration opposite. In dressage (classical riding) competitions measurements are given in meters, but here we will use feet. Any arena or open area will do. Simply adjust the distance between the letters. Also shown is one way to make a dressage letter. Two boards are joined at the top, making an upside-down V. Or, you can use a cone, a block or even a big empty plastic carton for each letter. Mark it clearly on opposite sides of whatever you use.

it will work for you and Primo. Maybe I'll read an article that makes me wonder if I've overlooked something basic during my lifetime with horses. I'll try to *mentally picture* it working. I might even test it on my own horses. They'll help me separate workable facts from "No way!"

Understanding Primo's Balance and Motion

The mechanics of motion have a direct effect on your riding. I'll explain this simply and briefly. (You may want to reread this section later on.)

First consider balance. As horsemen we use the terms "static balance" and "balance in motion."

Static balance refers to Primo's conformation, or how he is built. Imagine a straight line drawn to the ground from where you sit on Primo's back. As Primo stands relaxed, 60 percent of his weight is in front of that line and 40 percent is behind it. If you're sitting (preferably bareback) at the spot that's most comfortable for you, the 60-40 formula will hold true regardless of how Primo is put together. When your weight is added to Primo's back, things somehow come out 50-50.

We don't say Primo has "good static balance." We say he's "well balanced," which means he has a good body frame, straight legs and good muscular development.

Balance in motion is what Primo must constantly deal with as he moves forward. Think of how heavy his body is for each leg to support. Each time part of Primo's body passes forward and over these supporting legs, he loses his balance forward. He recovers it by moving his feet and other parts of his body to more effective locations. This is called counter-balancing. Primo does this at different speeds and to different degrees, depending on how fast he is moving. This is why his head bobs when he walks, stretches when he lopes but hardly moves when he jogs. Primo's feet move diagonally for the jog. This keeps his weight spread out evenly during all phases. He doesn't need to move his head for balance while his feet shift his weight from one corner to another. (Incidentally, Primo uses the same diagonal footfall for backing as he does for trotting. This makes it easier for him to keep his balance when he can't see where he's going.)

Primo deals with balance in motion when he moves sideways, too. Again, he does it by moving his feet and parts of his body. It'll be easier to see how he does this if we understand something about his withers and shoulders.

Primo's withers are made up of the spines of the second through the eighth thoracic vertebrae. These spines line up like slats in a picket fence. The "slats" lean backward, making a brace (like tent pegs) against the pull of the muscles in the crest of Primo's neck. This is how the withers anchor the neck. Because these spines are arched, they also form a fulcrum, so that when Primo lowers and stretches his neck, the muscles lying along his topline cause the center of his back to rise. He "rounds" his back.

These topline muscles are part of a fascinating series of bones, ligaments and tendons that work together to cause a horse to function. Dr. Deb Bennett refers to this interacting group as the "ring of muscles."

Although it looks like Primo's shoulders are part of his withers, they really are not. His shoulders are attached to his body and even to each other only by muscles and ligaments. He doesn't have collarbones, as we do. Each shoulder is attached to a foreleg, of course, but not to his spine. His rib cage is free to rock from side to side under the "bridge" of his shoulders.

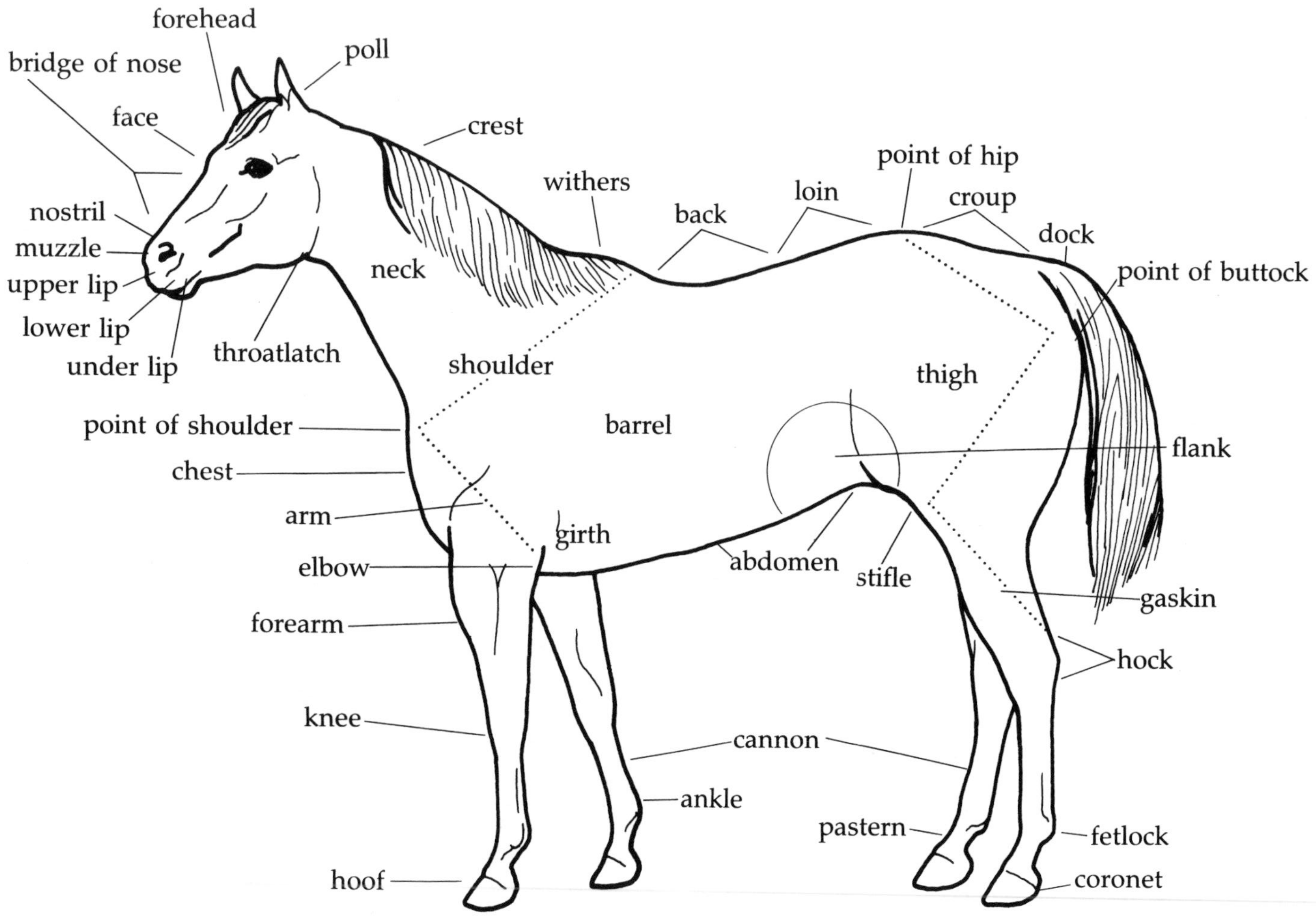

poll

forehead

bridge of nose

face

nostril

muzzle

upper lip

lower lip

under lip

crest

withers

throatlatch

neck

shoulder

point of shoulder

chest

arm

elbow

forearm

knee

hoof

back

loin

point of hip

croup

dock

barrel

girth

cannon

ankle

flank

point of buttock

thigh

stifle

abdomen

gaskin

hock

fetlock

coronet

pastern

Primo's Conformation

14

Consider another factor that is part of Primo's balance in motion: his *center of balance* (CB). When he stands still, his center of balance lies at the heaviest point inside his body, on a line that passes straight down through his chest cavity right behind the saddle horn. It's about on the 60-40 static balance line. But Primo's CB constantly changes position as he moves. It moves forward or backward as he adjusts to counterbalance his weight.

Primo's CB also moves from side to side. When he makes a quick turn, he has to lean to recover his balance. You might think, for example, that he bends around a barrel, but he doesn't. He can't. When weight in motion picks up speed, it also picks up vibrations. Nature made Primo's spine rigid to help keep him from jarring his bones and breaking them when his feet hit the ground. When he gallops around that barrel, he's not really bending his body. He's *tilting* it under the bridge of his shoulders. The muscles, tendons and ligaments in his legs, especially his pasterns (which do flex), handle an important role here.

Primo's center of balance constantly changes as he moves. When it moves ahead of its normal position, he becomes heavy on the forehand. This is fine when he's going fast, but not always so good when he's going slow. If he arches his neck and/or lowers his croup and works more off his hindquarters, this moves his CB rearward and lightens his forehand. You can see how this helps a cutting horse work a cow. Every time the cow tries to change directions, the horse is able to block an escape. He's balanced to switch his forehand lead fast.

Picture this. As Primo chases down a calf, his CB is forward and he is heavy on the forehand. This gives him speed. As soon as he moves into position for you to throw a rope,

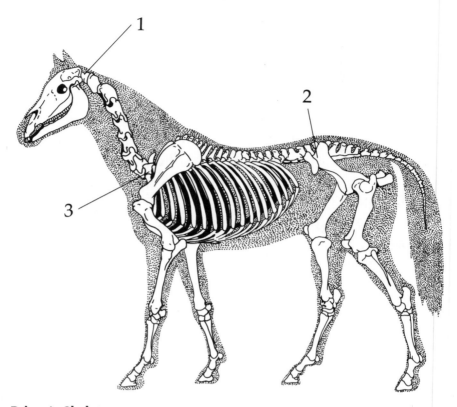

Primo's Skeleton

This skeleton is outlined with visible parts so you'll know where Primo's bones fit. (He has no bones in his ears or nose, for instance, and most of his neck and hindquarters are soft tissue.) The drawing is mainly to show some facts about his spine. Most horses have 31 vertebrae: 7 in the neck (cervical), 18 over the chest (thoracic), 6 in the loin (lumbar), 5 fused in the rump (sacrum) and 18 or so in the tail. A horse has 3 intervertebral joints designed for up-and-down bending: (1) The atlanto axial "head-neck" joint lets him flex at the poll. (2) The "big hinge" lumbosacral joint (between the last loin vertebra and the rump) allows his pelvis and hindquarters to rotate forward under his body. (3) The "chest joint" between the last cervical and first thoracic vertebra lets him raise and lower his neck, so he can graze. This joint also helps Primo keep in balance while moving.

he raises his head and drops his croup (sort of sits down). This shifts his CB and weight back. It also slows him. Now he's ready to bear the added weight of the calf when the

Primo's Withers
The shoulder/arm bone lines are dotted to show they are not
connected to his spine or ribs.

rope between it and the saddle horn is stretched. In fact, if
Primo didn't shift his weight and CB back, the calf's added
weight could pull him off his feet!

You now realize that weight and center of balance must
work as a team. And you've probably figured out that you,
Primo's rider, influence the location of his center of balance.
When mounted, you and Primo become one physical system. He must bear your added weight and distribute it in
some manner among his four legs. If you lean forward,
Primo's CB moves forward. If you lean back, Primo's CB is
moved to the rear. If you sit normally in a more forward
position, Primo will tend to be heavier on the forehand. If
you sit back more, he'll work more off his hindquarters. And
if you sit up straight, you'll encourage Primo to be more
centrally balanced. There is no *one* right way of sitting. It

depends on the activity. If Primo performs at a variety of tasks or classes, you'll need to adjust how you sit for each one.

We've discussed two of the factors that influence Primo's forward speed.

- What Primo does with his legs and body in order to keep his weight and center of balance in the right place for whatever he's doing.
- How your mounted position affects what Primo does.

There's one more important factor to consider:

- The ground surface over which Primo moves.

What Primo does with his legs gets a different result on different surfaces. For Primo to move forward, the ground surface must make a force forward and against the bottoms of Primo's feet. In other words, when Primo's feet push against the ground, the ground actually pushes back. This ground force is called friction. It is just as responsible for moving Primo forward as are the muscular and directional movements of his legs.

When Primo's feet push the ground, that's one solid pushing another solid. If he's swimming, his feet push water, which is less solid. He'll push faster but move slower than he'd move by pushing that fast on ground. Air is even less solid. If Primo were held in midair by a harness hooked to a helicopter, he would move his feet like crazy, trying to run away from a scary place! But his feet couldn't carry him because they are only pushing against air.

Different types of bearing surfaces have different degrees of push. Think of how it is for you to walk/run on ice, deep loose sand, packed sand or a sidewalk. You know how each one feels. Then think of the difference it makes if you wear tennis shoes or boots or go barefooted. Now think of Primo. Think of the surface he runs, slides and turns on. Think of him going barefoot—well trimmed, of course. Think of him wearing shoes that are big and slippery, shoes with grooves, shoes with studs or cleats and so forth. What he travels on and what he wears on his feet matter a lot.

CHAPTER 2

---◆◆◆---

So We'll Speak
the Same Language

Before we talk about riding a Western performance horse, let's go over some general information. You and I need to picture the same thing when I refer to it by name. I'm talking about basic things: your moves to communicate with Primo, his moves that respond to your moves, how he moves and why he acts a certain way.

If you read *Ride Western Style*, you'll already have learned some standard horse terms plus special ones of my own. But don't skip this chapter even if you read the other book. Besides getting a review, you'll find a lot of new material.

Primo's Senses and His Ways of Communicating

A horse's five natural senses are (1) sight, (2) hearing, (3) smell, (4) taste and (5) feel, meaning touch or contact. We humans have the same basic five natural senses, only ours are developed differently. What's important to a horse may not be so important to a human, and vice versa.

Primo's sense of feel is a very strong sense. Your sense of feel may not be as developed as his. But you can improve both Primo's sensitivity and your own. As a rider, you should work on this goal. It will help you communicate better with Primo. Your natural aids will be more effective.

Primo's vision works very differently from ours. Each of Primo's eyes sees a different picture, and each picture gets "reported" to a different half of his brain. (Each half works separately.) Primo sees more on each side when he faces forward than you can when you face forward, but he cannot focus on objects the way you can. His eyes are too far apart ever to blend both pictures into one sharp image. A piece of paper blown along the ground by the wind might, to Primo, look like an animal running. For the same reason, he can't see what's directly in front of his face or behind him (at his tail).

If Primo moves his head, then he can see whatever is directly in front or behind. Each eye sends a picture of what it sees to the opposite side of his brain. Left eye "talks" to right brain, and right eye "talks" to left brain. If you know about Primo's different manner of seeing, it may help you to understand and work out some problem you may have with him.

For example, suppose you have a problem loading Primo in a trailer. Perhaps the last time he was in it he saw something with one eye that really scared him. He wanted to get out of there or at least defend himself. But he couldn't do either because he was tied. If you were Primo, would you want to go into that scary trailer again?

Now that you understand why he doesn't want to load, you shouldn't force the issue. What Primo saw with eye A made him not want to enter the trailer. So the quickest way to get him over the problem could be to work with eye B first. Try loading him from the other side. The other eye didn't see whatever caused the problem, so that side of his brain won't have saved an old picture A to remind him of trouble A.

Primo's vision is the only one of his senses that functions in this way. So if Primo felt, smelled or tasted something he didn't like while he was trapped in the trailer, even though he only saw the problem with one eye, he'd still remember it.

Primo's vision is the least developed of his senses (rated by human standards, anyway), while his sense of touch is highly developed. Most experts say his sense of smell comes next, followed by taste, then hearing.

Later in this chapter I'll describe the natural aids, of which four are recognized. However, I list another aid that I call *think-talk*. Think-talk is both a sense and an aid. Both horse and rider must use think-talk, however, for it to function as an aid.

Primo has five recognized natural senses, so that makes think-talk his "sixth sense." No doubt you have heard of animals and people being described as having a sixth sense. It's not officially recognized, but it can't be denied. So a sixth sense is generally considered to be an instinct.

Feeling Primo's Footfalls

A horse moves forward by means of his gaits. Each gait has a definite pattern of footfalls, meaning the order in which each foot moves and strikes the ground. The typical Western horse uses three basic gaits: walk, trot and canter. Horses performing speed and reining events also use the gallop. Each gait has several variations in speed and manner of

walk

jog

lope

disunited lope

Gait Patterns

action. The jog, for instance, is a special slow trot, and the lope is a special slow canter. Both the jog and the lope are classic Western gaits.

It's easy to glance down at Primo's shoulders and tell which foot's up. Once you've learned the footfall pattern for

Primo's gaits, you can use that information to figure out where the rest of his feet are. But if you're serious about riding a performance horse, you'll also need to learn how to tell where Primo's feet are by feel. Your legs and seat can feel the motion and rhythm that happen whenever Primo's feet lift to move forward and drop to swing back.

I'll tell you how I learned to remember when a horse's feet land for each gait. This way should also help you feel Primo's feet. (It's easiest to feel when each back leg is lifted.) Before it makes sense, though, you must realize that Primo *pushes* his weight forward with his back feet and *pulls* it with his front feet. Diagonals mean that either his right rear foot and left front foot or his left rear foot and right front foot move at the same time. I speak of his inside and outside feet because it's easier to picture Primo's feet if you think of him traveling in a circle. His inside feet are the front and rear feet that are closer to the middle.

For a *walk*, think: "Outside push and pull rolls me to the inside push and pull, rolls me to the outside push and pull, rolls me to the inside push" and so forth. It may be easier to feel than "outside rear, outside front, inside rear, inside front."

For a *trot*, think of making an X: "First cross, second cross, first cross, second cross" and so forth. Or maybe "criss, cross, criss, cross." Diagonals are easy to feel.

For a *canter*, think: "Push across pull, push across pull" and so forth. It's far less complicated than "outside back, then inside back/outside front diagonals, then inside front." This way will also help you find that brief moment when all four of Primo's feet are in the air. Called the *period of suspension*, it happens when Primo's leading front foot leaves the ground and continues backward under his shoulder. In other words, it's right after the *pull* but before the next *push*.

We'll refer to this again, later on, when you learn ask a flying change of lead.

For a *gallop*, think: "Push a-cross pull, push a-cross pull" and so forth. (The word "a-cross" is broken up as a reminder that Primo's inside back foot lands slightly ahead of his outside front foot. They're almost, but not quite, diagonals.)

A cross-canter can be called a disunited canter, a crossfire or a missed lead. Don't mistake a cross-canter for a countercanter, though. They are not at all the same.

In a *countercanter*, Primo canters on the wrong lead on purpose, using the same footfall patterns as for a regular canter. It's a good test of Primo's obedience to your cues, but you need to know how to ask it properly and realize that it's harder for Primo to balance himself while he does it. A countercanter only applies to loping circles. Primo uses his outside lead to do it. He uses his right lead to circle to the left, and his left lead to circle to the right.

A *cross-canter* happens by mistake and, as you can see by the chart, follows a different footfall pattern. It's correct for a dog's lope but not a horse's. And it doesn't just happen while circling. To feel a cross-canter, think: "Push over pull, push over pull" and so forth. (Think "over" rather than "across" because Primo goes *over* and uses both feet on the same side instead of going *across* using diagonals. That's why this gait is rougher than a canter.)

Let's sum up the gait footfall memory helpers:

Walk—outside push and pull rolls me to the inside push and pull, etc.

Trot—make an X with first cross, second cross, etc.

Canter—push across pull, etc.

Gallop—push a-cross pull, etc.

Cross-canter—push over pull, etc.

Primo's Gaits: Their Various Speeds

Primo's natural gaits are walk, trot, canter and gallop. Each gait's footfall pattern should keep repeating itself, even though each gait has several different speeds and various ways for Primo to perform it. So you can always use the gait footfall memory helpers to locate his feet.

Start with Primo's walk. Most riders don't spend enough time on their horse's walk. Whether schooling or showing, they tend to treat the walk as a rest period for the horse and themselves. This is a big mistake. Probably close to half of everything that Primo does, in a show ring or elsewhere, is based upon his walk.

Just as Primo needs a good walk, you need to develop a feel for the sequence of Primo's feet while he performs it. Knowing where his feet are helps you lengthen or collect his stride and develop good square halts. For example, you'll also work on his turns on the haunches from the walk and ask for prompt canter departures on the correct lead from the walk.

The American Quarter Horse Association (AQHA) and the American Paint Horse Association (APHA) define the Western walk as "a natural, flat-footed, four-beat gait. The horse must move straight and true at the walk. The walk must be alert, with a stride of reasonable length in keeping with the size of the horse." The rules of other associations use very similar words to describe the walk.

There are three speeds for the Western walk:

1. A *free walk*, also called a slow walk (3 to 4 miles per hour), is casual and undriven. It should only be allowed for taking a rest break or for letting Primo pick his way through unfamiliar surroundings.

2. A *medium walk*, also called an ordinary walk, is relaxed but faster (4 to 6 miles per hour). In other words, you don't allow Primo to creep along half asleep. This is the walk you use in the show ring and for most schooling. Hunter Under Saddle and other English show rules define it as a "natural" gait that "must be alert, with a stride of reasonable length in keeping with the size of the horse."

3. Speed varies for the *fast walk*. This is a useful exercise for encouraging Primo to obey your leg signals and stretch out as fast as he can without breaking into a trot.

Primo has three distinct speeds at the trot:

1. A *jog* (4 to 6 miles per hour) is the classic Western trot. Its shortened stride makes it easy for you to sit.

   AQHA defines the jog as "a smooth, ground-covering two-beat diagonal gait. The horse works from one pair of diagonals to the other pair. The jog should be square, balanced and with a straight, forward movement of the feet. Horses walking with their back feet and trotting on the front are not considered performing the required gait. When asked to extend the jog, he moves out with the same smooth way of going." APHA uses the same definition, except for calling it the *jog-trot*.

2. The ordinary *trot* (7 to 8 miles per hour) has a longer stride and higher leg action. It's what the judge usually has in mind when he asks for the jog to be extended. The ordinary trot is used in English classes, where the rider is asked to post. Sometimes it's called a long trot.

3. A faster *extended trot* (9 to 10 miles per hour), is a leg-strengthening exercise for Primo and you. It's also sometimes called a long trot.

Here are Primo's speeds at the canter:

1. The *lope* is a slow (7 to 8 miles per hour) rhythmic Western gait with a shortened stride.

   The AQHA and APHA define the lope as "an easy, rhythmical three-beat gait. Horses moving to the left should lope on the left lead. Horses moving to the right should lope on the right lead. Horses traveling at a four-beat gait are not considered to be performing at a proper lope. The horse should lope with a natural stride and appear relaxed and smooth. He should be ridden at a speed that is a natural way of going."

2. A regular *canter* is faster (10 to 12 miles per hour) than the lope. The stride should be long, low and ground covering. It's the canter used in English classes unless more speed is asked for. "More speed" means a hand gallop.

3. A *hand gallop* (14 to 16 miles per hour) is still a canter, not a true gallop. In AQHA Hunter classes it's described as "a definite lengthening of the stride with a noticeable difference in speed. The horse should be under control at all times and be able to halt in a smooth, balanced manner."

Primo's true *gallop* ranges from 16 to 22 miles per hour for arena events (how fast depends on which event), and he can reach 35 miles per hour on a racetrack.

Horseman's Terms

Horse people use terms, just as baseball or medical people do, so they can communicate with each other easily. A good example is *rubbernecking*, which describes a horse that is overflexing (tucking his chin way back toward his chest) to avoid the bit. Most terms and even slang phrases paint such a clear picture that you won't need my help in understanding them.

Topline means the outline of Primo's top parts, from his ears to his tail, viewed from the side.

A *transition* means what happens, or what is used, while changing from one thing to another. (It's the B between changing from A to C.) It's often used to describe changing from one gait to another. These are simple examples: Primo makes an upward transition from a walk to a trot and a downward transition from a walk to a halt.

A *stride* is what Primo does over and over while he moves at any gait. It refers more to action than pattern.

The term *disengagement* describes how far Primo's rear leg swings ahead of the vertical (meaning where his leg is when he stands square) and how far it swings behind the vertical. The term doesn't include his front legs. But, technically, all legs are engaged when they swing forward and disengaged when they swing back. Think of horizontal as front to back (rather than side to side, in this case) and vertical as up to down. Now, if Primo is horizontally disengaged, we say he's *strung out*. If he's vertically engaged (collected, in other words), he's *pulled together*.

A *soft-sided* horse responds to the least amount of pressure from the rider's leg. This horse will "give in" to the rider's leg by moving to the side opposite the one that's getting pressure. He's *even sided* if he'll respond to pressure from either side and doesn't prefer one side.

If Primo shows *impulse*, that means he is alert, keen and willing, that he appears to have a whole lot of energy stored up but he's obediently waiting for you to ask for it.

You want Primo to be *straight* whether he's moving in a

straight line or in a circle. He needs to be straight for quick halts and for backing, too. Being straight, also called riding on the line, means Primo's body and spine are evenly loaded on his legs. He's not cocked to one side, front or back. He looks in the direction he moves (except when backing). When moving in a straight line or in a circle, Primo's back feet follow the same line as his front feet.

Actually, his feet make two lines by going straight. If he's not moving straight, then they make three or even four lines.

Stabilized refers to Primo's speed at any gait. He's stabilized (or evenly rated) if he stays at the same speed you ask (no slower, no faster) until he's asked to change.

Finally, here are some terms that apply to Primo and his bit. We say Primo is *above the bit* if he carries his head too high or sticks his nose up in an effort to escape the bit's control. Being *behind the bit* means rubbernecking, which I've already described. This usually happens as a result of bad training that should have taught him to flex his head in a collected way. Primo responds to you properly when he *accepts the bit* (is *up in the bridle*).

How Build Affects Riding

A boy's bone structure is different from that of a girl. I will explain how these structural differences can cause boys and girls to function differently in the saddle.

As the drawings show, the main difference is found in the pelvis. This difference exists, regardless of age, size or weight. The tailbone and thigh bones differ, too. Pelvic differences create other differences between boys and girls that show up in the knees and ankles. Once you're aware of these differences, you could probably look at a skeleton and tell if it is that of a male or a female.

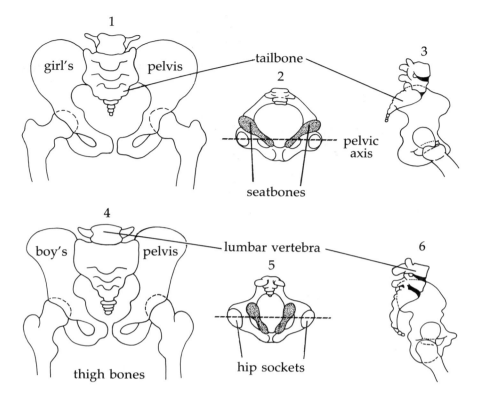

1 girl's pelvis

tailbone

2

pelvic axis

3

seatbones

4 boy's pelvis

lumbar vertebra

5

6

thigh bones

hip sockets

Pelvis Comparisons

The top row shows the pelvis of a girl, the bottom row shows the pelvis of a boy. Drawings 1 and 4 show the front view. With a boy and girl of nearly equal size, the girl's pelvis, especially the center opening, is wider than the boy's. Because her pelvis is wider, her thighbones slant slightly inward. Therefore her knees are at a different angle and her feet hang down differently from a boy's. A boy's thigh bones come down nearly straight from his narrow hips. There is a difference in a boy's and a girl's tailbone, as you can see in drawings 3 and 6. The middle drawings (2 and 5) "look up" at the pelvis sitting in the saddle. They show the difference in the pelvis centers and in the seatbones (darkened to stand out). A girl's seatbones fan out quite a bit. A boy's seatbones are nearly parallel. The line that passes through the hip sockets shows where the pelvic axis crosses. It crosses almost at the middle of a boy's seatbones, but it crosses more to the front of a girl's seatbones. A girl "wants" to balance more forward. However, she can make changes with her abdominal muscles to control this situation. Drawings 3 and 6 compare the angles, especially the tailbone, in a balanced seat (neither tipped forward nor flexed down and back).

A boy is built so that his pelvis wants to sit squarely balanced. It's also easy for him to rock back and use his tailbone like a stool. The way a girl's tailbone is shaped, she balances more comfortably by rolling her pelvis slightly forward. It's natural for her to want to sit swaybacked.

It would seem that a boy is naturally built for riding Western style and that a girl is naturally built for riding English style. But neither sitting on a stool nor sitting swaybacked is correct position for either style of riding. There is, however, more than one correct way to sit. We'll discuss good seat in detail later on.

When riding without stirrups, a boy's feet hang nearly level, while a girl's relaxed feet point more downward and inward. Although a girl's heels are naturally raised higher than a boy's, her flexibility makes it easier for her to rotate her ankles and let her heels drop to a proper stirrup position. Boys tend to have stiffer ankles. Both boys and girls need to stretch those leg tendons that raise and lower the heel. Nicely stretched tendons let your heels drop naturally when your foot rests in the stirrup. Forcing your heels down makes your ankles stiff. The easiest way to stretch your ankle tendons is to draw circles with your toes. The bigger and rounder and more to the outside you can make your circles, the more flexible your ankles will be. You can practice this exercise while sitting or lying down. It's also a good way to loosen ankles that become stiff from being in the stirrup too long. Just slip your foot out of the stirrup and draw circles with it.

Here's another exercise that you can do when you're not on Primo. It's great for developing strength and balance in your legs and ankles. It also helps develop strength and control in your abdomen and lower body.

- Stand on a stair step with the balls of your feet on the step. Let your heels hang over the edge.
- When you can hold that position steady, you're ready to sink your heels and do knee bends. Hold the rail or wall only if you're in danger of falling. Otherwise, put your arms out to the sides ("airplane") or straight forward.

Back to bones. A boy's hip socket is shaped so that it's easier for him to sit smoothly during Primo's faster gaits than it is for most girls. The angle that a boy's thigh bone makes with his pelvis makes it easier for him to rest the inner surface of his thighs flat against the saddle, to keep his knees close to the saddle without squeezing and to point his toes forward.

Girls can make up for bone differences by their special ability to control their muscles, especially the iliopsoas (ill-e-o-*so*-us), the big posture muscle in the abdomen. Girls can use it to adjust their tailbone so that they won't sit swaybacked.

The easiest way to describe how this muscle can be used is to imagine what you'd do if someone were about to hit you below the belt with his fist. You'd harden the muscles in your lower abdomen for protection. At the same time, also tuck your "tail" like you would for protection from a spanking.

Meanwhile, relax. Any time you concentrate on flexing various muscles for riding, try to keep your belly and chest areas as relaxed as possible. *Breathe from your belly*, not from the top of your lungs. Proper breathing is very important for both girls and boys, especially while active.

Girls can use muscles in their thighs and buttocks to relax

the angle of their hip joints (where the thigh bones connect to the pelvis). By relaxing certain muscles, girls can actually widen their "grip of hip" angle.

To get an idea of what I mean—plus the feel of how to do it—picture how a pair of pliers works. It can pick up a pin when the joint is at one end of the slot. It can also pick up a much wider object, but only after you slide the joint to the opposite end of the slot. Now transfer what works for getting a wider grip with pliers to what works for getting a wider grip with hip joints. A girl can "pick up" a deeper seat on Primo by first relaxing her hip joints. This lets them "slide" open wider, which places her thigh bones more upright. This, in turn, lets her thighs and knees assume angles more like a boy's. Riding without stirrups is a good exercise for widening your grip.

While we're still picturing pliers, it's easier to sit in a forward seat by using your muscles to "slide the joint" ever so slightly toward the other end. Tightening your "pliers nut" like this gives you better leverage for using your legs. It gives more strength to your thighs for carrying additional weight. Both a normal and a deep seat are three-pointed. Your weight is shared by your seat and each leg. But a forward seat can be three- or two-pointed. For a three-pointed forward seat, you lean forward and roll up on your seatbones. But you still sit. A two-pointed position is when you straddle above (rather than sit on) the saddle. Your legs balance your full weight in motion as you keep up with Primo's motion.

Natural Aids

Your hands, legs, body and voice are called natural aids for riding.

Your *hands* control the reins. They're also used to discipline Primo (by reins or whip) if he does not obey and to praise him with a loving pat after he's done a good job. "Good hands" is the standard by which horsemen are judged.

Your *legs* (including your seatbones and your feet) are used to guide and push Primo. They're also used for keeping your own balance.

Leg pressure means pressing in with your calves. Depending on how and when it's used, it can tell Primo to

- turn
- move sideways
- go faster
- slow down
- back up

Brace with your calves (no squeezing) to stop Primo. Pressure from your seatbone (usually thigh, too) is for

- turning
- leg yielding
- controlling Primo's speed (fast, slow or steady)

Use your heel (with or without a spur) only in cases where your leg pressure is ignored. Use it to ask Primo for

- more speed
- more energy
- a longer stride
- a turn

Your *body* is used to guide and drive Primo. He responds to feeling your shifted weight. That's why I'll sometimes refer to your weight rather than your body as an aid (or cue or signal). Your body also "reads" Primo's body signals.

When it comes to controlling Primo and reading his moves, it's hard to tell where your seatbones leave off and the rest of your body begins. You use your legs and body together most of the time, anyway.

You communicate with Primo by way of feel when you use your hands, legs and body. Communication works both ways. These aids allow you and Primo to signal each other.

Remember these facts when using "feel" signals:

- Most Western horses are trained to move away from one or more *prompt* contacts with pressure. But it's natural for a horse to *lean into steady pressure*. Apply this principle to aids given by your hand and leg. Remember that your leg can include your seatbone.
- In order to keep in balance, Primo will want to move himself to keep your weight centered on his back. That's why you can use your shifted body weight as an aid.
- Whether riding with a loose rein or with more contact, you'll balance Primo between your legs and your hands. Your legs control his back end. Your hands control his front end. Your body keeps both ends in harmony.
- If you use more than one signal, make sure they fit together. Sometimes your signals need to close every door except one. What you want Primo to do must clearly be the only door left open.

Your *voice* encourages and calms Primo. It's also used to get his attention or to give a command. You can use animallike sounds (cluck, kiss, hiss, growl) and words. (Short, distinct words work better.) Primo learns voice commands by association. He matches sound A or word A with situation A. Therefore, do not use the same sound or word for more than one purpose. For example, "Whoa" is overused. It should only be used to make Primo stop moving. "Easy" could slow him down and "Steady" could get him to relax. Avoid commands that sound alike but are used for different reasons. "No" sounds too much like "Whoa." Use "Stop it" or "Quit" instead of "No" to mean "Don't do that." Or make up your own clear commands.

Think-Talk

Now we come to the extra natural aid, the one I call *think-talk*. Some people call it nonverbal communication or visualization. Not everybody agrees that it works both ways, but I feel that it does. With think-talk, a horse and rider communicate mentally. They can exchange information.

The idea of think-talk is this: You send Primo a mental picture of what you want him to do. It must be a positive picture, not a negative one. For example, you're riding Primo at a walk up the center of the arena toward two marker cones. One is on your right, the other's on your left. Without moving any part of yourself as a "feel" aid, you send Primo a picture of him carrying you at a walk to the cone on the left and then stopping. This is a clear and simple example. You might want to try it as a test of your ability to use think-talk with Primo. If you're pleased with the results, give Primo a big hug. You're *both* lucky!

A negative picture would look like the positive one *except* that you'd be thinking it's *not* what you want.

Primo wouldn't understand your negative approach. It's too complicated. He could understand your "Stop it!" right after he tried to bite or kick, but that's the normal limit to his negative I.Q. Besides, "Stop it!" would be a direct *positive* response then. And you'd add a quick hard slap.

If you don't want Primo to go to the left cone, don't even bring up the subject. Find a positive way to let Primo know what you want him to do. Always think a picture of him (and you) doing the right thing. Other than for reasons of "Stop it!" discipline, train yourself to think positive. It's an easier way to "think like a horse."

Here's an example of another kind of negative think-talk. While riding a trail class, you think: I hope Primo won't mess up backing through the L. So he messes up. You should think-talk of him backing through the L perfectly.

Think-talk works for things besides riding. You can use it any time you need to talk with your horse. When you're on the ground where he can see you, you have the advantage of adding body-talk. Briefly, body-talk includes gestures you can make with your body that are similar to gestures he uses to say things to you, to other horses or to another animal. This language is communicated by how and where you move your head, shoulder, hip, hand or foot, for example. Of course, you have to use something else to say what Primo says with his ears and tail. Use your voice.

Even those who refuse to acknowledge nonverbal communication *use think-talk anyway.* However, they don't accept the part about mental picture-passing between horse and rider. They say when a rider "thinks the picture of" (visualizes) what he does, this helps him or her in other ways. For example, if you look and think "right" when you want Primo to go to the right, they say you're more likely to do everything with the hands / legs / body "feel" aids that a rider *should* do for asking Primo to turn to the right. Whatever *they* believe or call this, it's think-talk.

I also believe think-talk works both ways. Primo's message might come across as an urge, an unvoiced hunch or feeling about something that wasn't already on your mind. For example, if Primo is very thirsty but his good training keeps him from heading for the nearest water hole while he's under saddle, you might come up with the great idea of riding him over to the water hole and letting him drink.

Artificial Aids and Rider Safety

The artificial aids for riding include whips, spurs, tie-downs, draw reins and other devices that either force Primo to do something or keep him from doing something. A *whip* or *spurs* can be used to discipline Primo or to reinforce your command for action. *Draw reins* (and other devices, including homemade ones) are training tools that can teach Primo how to position his head. A *tie-down* will help you keep Primo from tossing his head to avoid the bit. But a tie-down can also help Primo keep his balance while quickly "shifting gears" during roping and barrel racing. Used correctly, artificial aids are helpful because they reinforce natural aids. Used wrongly, they are barbaric!

Chaps technically are not a riding aid because they're not used on Primo. They're more of a rider's safety aid because chaps can help you hold your position in the saddle.

Gloves are another safety aid. They help keep your hands warm in cold weather, which is important because hands don't function as well when they're cold. Gloves can also keep the reins from slipping and protect you from rope burns. If you wear gloves that are designed for riding, you won't lose feel of the reins.

Boots can vary in height, material, design, quality and cost. From a safety viewpoint, look for the following:

- Enough heel to keep your foot from sliding too far into the stirrup.
- Enough leather to protect you from bruises caused by rubbing the stirrups or fenders.
- Enough room so you can flex your ankle and calf. (Some boot tops pinch or confine your leg.)

I prefer short, plain leather, flat-heeled, round-toed ropers. Ropers are designed like traditional English boots except they're not as high-topped. (You can also get lace-up ropers, like paddock shoes.) They come in many colors, usually cost less than boots with pointy toes, and are easy to clean. Spurs stay in place better on ropers, too. There's no curved high heel for them to slide down.

Also until recently, people who wanted to protect their heads while riding Western style had to wear English-style hard hats. The Lexington safety helmet pictured in this book is the first Western-style head protection product to meet current ASTM safety standards. Whether you use this hat or another kind, please protect your head by wearing a *safety helmet*. Wear it for all "contact" horse activities. This includes loading Primo into the trailer or taking him out.

Ways to Use the Reins

You should ride well enough by now to know more than one way to use the reins. Unless you read *Ride Western Style*, we may not know these ways by the same names.

- *Neck rein*, also called bearing rein, is the classic Western way to turn a horse while riding one-handed. (It's also used for polo and foxhunting.) Lay the rein against one side of Primo's neck. He'll respond by turning in the other direction. For example, if you lay the rein against the left side of his neck, he'll turn right.

- For a *direct rein*, the pulled rein on either side works directly from mouth to rear. In two-handed riding, you use a direct rein to turn Primo without moving your hand away to the side. You pull the left rein to turn left, the right rein to turn right. Direct reining is also used to stop and to back Primo. Most of the time, you'll ride one-handed and pull evenly with both reins. The main thing to remember is that a direct rein is pulled straight back (or up and back).

- A *leading rein* is also called an opening rein or a plow rein. You ride two-handed to use it. It's similar to direct reining in that the rein is pulled from either side of Primo's neck. The difference is that a leading rein is pulled out to the side. For example, you "lead" Primo to the left by a left rein. The rein "opens" the door on the left for him to move through. (Actually what opens is the angle between the rein and Primo's neck.)

  The leading rein is handy for training, but it's also used on a finished horse for some activities. For example, barrel racers lead their galloping horses around barrels.

- An *indirect rein* is applied somewhat like a neck rein. You put the rein against Primo's neck or sometimes against his shoulder. The main difference is that an indirect rein is never used alone. Usually it controls the off side, not the leading side. When riding two-handed, you can use an indirect rein on one side to make minor corrections. The rein on the other side gives your main cue. With an indirect rein you can ask Primo to shift his weight from one side or the other for making perfect circles and turns. Or you can use it as a reminder not to drift away from the rail. The indirect rein is a handy training tool you'll use sooner or later, whether riding a green or a finished horse.

- The *pulley rein* is an emergency brake. You grab one rein up short and press that hand hard against Primo's neck. At the same time, you really pull back and up with the other rein. Another version is the crossover. With it, you cross both reins into a strong sliding "see-saw" against a runaway's neck. But let's hope you'll never have to use this on Primo.

Bailing Out

Usually you'll realize when you've lost your seat and are going off. The information given below and the photographs on pages 43 to 45 make clear how to control your fall from the left side of the horse.

- Lean forward and grasp Primo's mane firmly while you *slide or kick both feet out of the stirrups.*
- For going off to the left, bring your right leg over Primo's back, and then vault off. This is like a regular vaulting dismount, except that you must push off stronger with both hands in front. Then arch your back more to raise your right leg so it can clear the cantle. Put your right hand wherever it helps most but not where it can be trapped as you vault over. Your right leg is easier to control if you straighten your knee and point your toes as you would for diving.
- Push against Primo with your left hand as you go off.

This gets your legs clear of his body and saddle so your feet can drop freely to the ground.

- Keep your right hand or arm in contact with Primo's body or the saddle. This hug keeps you from going too far away from Primo after pushing and will also slow your slide.
- Slide down Primo's shoulder and land on your feet, facing the same way as Primo. Bend your knees to absorb the shock of landing.
- Take a step or two forward to keep up with Primo. He'll probably slow down and stop as soon as he feels you go off. If you can't keep hold of him, then push yourself away.

When you bail out on the right side, follow the same directions but do everything "right" instead of "left."

Practice bailing out first from a standstill, both sides, then add speed. Don't overdo it, however. Too much practice will teach Primo to anticipate. He'll stop any time he feels you shift your weight like you would before vaulting off. Unless he's used for roping, and this is what you want him to do, it can be quite annoying.

CHAPTER 3

———◆◈◆———

Horse Shows in General, Pleasure Classes in Particular

The logical first move from pleasure riding into the show ring is by way of pleasure classes. That's where most competitors start out. Some competitors even make Western pleasure a specialty and collect championships. In Western Pleasure and Hunter Under Saddle (one Western, the other English) Primo is judged on his performance, condition and conformation. Unlike other performance events, nothing fancy is asked of Primo in pleasure classes. But he is expected to do a good job of the basics.

Show Ring Philosophy

A judge can pick out those riders who've done their homework. The rider who gets the judge's attention from the moment he or she comes through the in-gate has a certain look.

That look says, "I've prepared for this moment. I've read the rules for this class about a hundred times and studied winning rides. Primo and I have practiced what we're supposed to do here. We can do it without getting mad at each other, too. My folks are careful about money, but Primo wears the nicest show tack we can afford. That's why I take such good care of it. We also put a lot of time and thought into what I'm wearing. And Judge, you wouldn't *believe* all the work I put in on Primo's mane, tail, coat and hooves! I spend almost as much time making him beautiful as I do riding him. Take a good look, Judge. We're the best!''

You *need* that ''We're the best!'' (WTB) look. You may have heard the song that begins ''Whenever I feel afraid . . .'' from *The King and I*. The words of that song say what I'm saying here. While you'll only *think* and not *whistle* your merry tune, you definitely should hold your head erect. In other words, use think-talk on yourself. Leave your case of show jitters at the in-gate and go ride.

You may say, ''But I thought it was Primo, not me, who's supposed to be judged in Western Pleasure class.'' Or maybe you're showing Primo in Hunter Under Saddle, an English pleasure class performed on the flat (no jumping).

Technically, Primo is the contestant and you are the exhibitor. However, you do each reflect the other, regardless of who's being judged. Each makes the other look better or worse. You're partners, remember?

The Importance of Rule Books

In an event where Primo is being judged, he could be doing exactly what you ask him to do and be doing a great job of it. Yet he might not win unless you followed all the rules for that event. He might even be disqualified because of a silly mistake you made.

Before you can play any game, you need to know the

rules. Buy a rule book and read it. Make sure it's recent. Rules change. Generally, they aren't changed until after something has been going on for a while in the show world. (We call that something a trend.) Trends are given a trial period during which they're carefully studied and discussed between judges and rule committee members. During this trial, a contestant isn't supposed to win or lose because of the trend. If, after the trial period—usually at least a year— the trend seems good, then a new rule is added or an existing rule is changed to include it. If the trend seems harmful or unfair, then a rule is added or changed to clearly forbid it. Also, some rules may get rewritten in order to be made perfectly clear. (Officials refer to these rewrites as "housekeeping" changes.)

Each year, newly added or changed rules are shaded in the rule books so you can see what's different. It's even better to have the current year's rule book *and* the last year's. If anybody tries to tell you a "fact" that no longer applies, you'll be able to track down the truth. This is one reason why you should carry your rule book or books to a show. (Put your name on the cover where it can clearly be seen, so it can be returned to you if you lend or lose it.)

Be sure your rule book is from the correct association (or associations) sponsoring an event. Some rules are unbending and universal, other rules differ. It depends on who runs the show. If registered by breed, Primo might belong to the American Quarter Horse Association (AQHA), the American Paint Horse Association (APHA), the Appaloosa Horse Club, Inc. (ApHC), the International Arabian Horse Association (IAHA), the American Morgan Horse Association, Inc. (AMHA), or one of several others. Maybe he's registered by color. He could, for example, belong to the Palomino Horse Association (PHA) or the American Buckskin Horse Association (ABHA). Some groups are for performance. They include the American Horse Show Association (AHSA), the National Cutting Horse Association (NCHA), the National Reining Horse Association (NRHA) and others, many of which are listed in the Appendix.

Show Terms

Here are some frequently used show terms and their definitions:

- A *working event* refers to an event where each horse/rider entry performs individually. Examples are reining, cutting, trail and barrel racing.
- A *class event* refers to more than one contestant riding in the ring at the same time, such as Western Pleasure. "Class" can also mean the total number of contestants entered in an event.
- *Youth* refers to a rider who is eighteen years or younger. For show purposes, your age as of January 1 is your age all year long. Major shows that expect many entries will divide the classes. For three classes there's 11 and under, 12 to 14 and 15 to 18. For two classes there's 13 and under and 14 to 18, and for small shows it's combined, 18 and under. A youth class may also be called a *junior division*, referring to the riders.
- *Open*, when referring to riders, means open to all riders. This includes youth plus adult amateurs and professionals. Sometimes it's good for you to ride Primo in an open class. When referring to horses, "open" can mean open to all breeds or open to all ages and backgrounds of training / showing.

- *Senior* refers to the horse being five years or older.
- *Junior* refers to the horse being four years or younger. There can also be classes for horses two years and under, but I'll assume Primo is older and not cover those rules here. Some performance horses are finished and dependable by the time they're four years old. (They "have a good handle.")
- If a snaffle bit is allowed, the rules say "snaffle bit." For Western classes, only junior horses may be shown on the snaffle bit or bosal, both of which may be ridden two-handed. Otherwise, the term "bit" means a curb bit, having a solid or broken mouthpiece, shanks and a curb strap or acceptable chain. Senior Western horses must be shown on a bit and ridden one-handed in classes where rein-holding rules apply. Riders of junior horses have a choice.

All rule books describe suitable and unacceptable tack items.

Pleasing the Judge

You've seen styles of clothes, popular music and even celebrities pass in and out of fashion. Certain horse show fashions change with the times, too. They may also differ according to where you live. Therefore, you'll do better at showing Primo if you visit several shows in your area and study what goes on before you compete.

A few years ago, most judges wanted a pleasure horse to move fairly fast along the rail. More recently, the winning look focused on "relaxation." The horse carried his head very low, kept his tail tucked like he expected to be whipped across his rump and barely lifted his feet. Some people deliberately put their show prospects through stress and even pain to get them to move and look like a few champions did naturally. The less talented horses ended up moving in an artificial manner. Now, thank goodness, we're back to a more natural way of moving. No more "anteaters" moping around the show ring. Rule books say a horse should appear relaxed and happy, move naturally and be alert to what his rider asks. He should appear pleasurable to ride.

Judging is a serious job and all horse show judges must follow certain procedures in order to be permitted to judge. (Men and women judge, but here I'll just use "he" instead of "he or she.")

- An applicant for a judge's card must supply the names of other reputable horsemen within the particular association (AQHA, AHSA, for example). The applicant must be recommended by confidential responses from these credible persons to the association before he's even considered.
- Next, he must attend a judges' clinic and score well on several difficult tests to prove he knows what to look for in the show ring.
- If he passes everything, he gets a card.
- In order to keep the card, he has to travel, judge a certain number of shows and attend clinics each year. If he doesn't do a good job, he's not asked to judge other shows. Most rule books devote several pages to what a judge can and cannot do.

Overall, judges always have and always will look for a balanced and happy horse that moves well. Some, however, tend to look harder for certain things. One judge might consider a horse's topline more important than his leg action or speed. Another judge might prefer to view the action from a certain spot in the arena. He might prefer to stand more in a corner than in the middle, for instance. Or, he might tend to work his classes longer.

This is not ignoring the rules. It's more a matter of how a judge likes to decide on matters for which the rule book allows him some individual flexibility. Some judges might even look closer at a particular horse because of the trainer's reputation or the horse's ancestors. But a great judge won't be misled by fancy trimmings. If he sees a horse and/or rider of unknown background give a brilliant performance, he'll give credit where credit is due. He'll pick that talented-but-unknown team over the horse and rider having less talent but bearing a "big name."

All in all, your best policy is to believe that the judge watching you and Primo perform is honest and capable.

Some Pre-Showtime Information

Before you make any further plans to show Primo, you need to find out whether he qualifies. If it's a breed show, you need to show proof of his registration and ownership. This is not something you can get overnight. The paperwork takes time, possibly several months. You'll also need a current membership card and, of course, current rule book.

Another matter that needs to be taken care of long before show day is Primo's health. Surely you do a good job of this all along, but you need to be extra careful with a show horse. The excitement that is part of showing tends to stress horses. When they're stressed, they get sick more easily. Primo could pick up something bad from another horse. He might even colic. Tell your vet what you plan to do with Primo. Make sure he's up to date on his shots and deworming program. Check to see if he needs a Coggins test. Try to have the farrier see Primo about a week before showtime. Bring hay and grain from home, along with a supply of the water that he's used to drinking.

After you arrive and get Primo settled in, see the show manager. If you've prepaid your fees, they'll check your name and give you a number. Otherwise, you'll pay your entry fees and get a number then. Whether it's Primo or you being judged, the number is assigned to Primo. Secure the number to an easily visible spot. Pin it to the back of your jacket or shirt, or pin it on Primo's blanket (fairly high and behind your thigh).

Nearly all shows allow late ("post") entries. This gives you an opportunity to show Primo in classes you hadn't planned on entering until after you arrived and saw who was there and what was going on. Cut-off time varies according to how big the show is, but most don't stop posting entries until it's nearly time for that class to start.

If it's an individual event, numbers are drawn to determine who goes first, second and so on. This usually happens fairly close to class time. That way, there's less possibility of a last-minute "scratch" (advising officials that you cannot or will not ride) or a "no-show" (not showing up to ride).

Usually it's better to combine classes rather than have just one or two entries. For one reason, the winners score more points if the classes are larger. You want as many points as possible for award honors.

Most scratches and no-shows are the result of poor planning by the rider. He or she didn't allow enough time between events to get ready. The show moves faster when classes are combined. Be aware of this possibility if you decide to post-enter. Getting ready for a class involves preparing yourself *mentally* as well as making any changes in Primo's tack or in your attire.

Class Begins

Enter the ring at a walk, usually with the rail on your right side. If it's different, you'll be told ahead of time. Remember the WTB look I described under Show Ring Philosophy? That's the think-talk you'll use as you enter the ring. (Maybe it'll work on the judge, too!)

Some riders practically break their necks to keep their eye on the judge. If they see that the judge is looking at them, they'll flash a big smile or else pop into a pleasure-riding posture that's too stern and artificial.

Your head weighs ten to twenty pounds. Shifting it in any direction affects the balance of your weight. If you turn your head to watch the judge, Primo can feel this and respond in a way you don't want (unless you want to turn).

I'm not suggesting that you ignore the judge. If you can make eye contact with him and give a friendly smile without turning your head around to do so, that's great. You certainly want to be aware of the judge. But you also want to be aware of other things. You need to concentrate on Primo at all times (more on that later). At the same time, you need to be tuned in to the other horses and riders and to the announcer. There's a chain of communication between the judge (or judges) and announcer that may involve several people. You don't have to concern yourself with those people, but you do need to listen for the announcer's instructions. He'll tell you when to change gaits, when to reverse, when to line up and so forth. Don't just copy what you see the other riders doing. If you waited that long to make your move, the judge probably saw it and marked you down.

Another group of important people need to be reckoned with. I'm referring to your family, friends and coach (if you have one). A good coach knows how to support a student and how to avoid distractions. A good coach won't rattle a student's self-confidence before, during or after a class. Family and friends new to showing may have to learn through experience when to cheer and when to keep their mouths shut. Consider your family and friends on your side, but part of the background. It's more important now for you to concentrate on what's going on in the ring.

Most riders get nervous the first time they compete at a show. They worry about their riding ability. (You can ride as well if not better in the show ring as you can at home . . . provided you convince yourself you can do it.) They wonder, "Can I can ride as well as the others?" (If you learn from this book, you'll ride *at least* as well as most.) They worry about how they'll look. (Some ideas on what to wear are at the end of this chapter.)

They worry because of the unknown.

Now we reach the heart of the problem. Not knowing what to expect is a major cause of show jitters. The best solution is to visit some local shows before you compete with Primo. Mentally practice the routine of listening for instructions and obeying them. Imagine yourself as one of the riders—ideally, the best rider. This kind of think-talk ahead of time is an easy way to pick up the feel of showing. It will settle your nerves so that, once you're in the ring, you won't waste your energy or attention on the wrong things. Think about what your WTB look told the judge as you rode in. If you make a mistake, don't get upset. Perhaps you can make up for it. Besides, there's always a next time.

Routine for a Western Pleasure Class

A pleasure class is a contest to find the most mannerly horse for doing basic fundamentals. Primo should be quiet and composed at all times. You need to know how to sit, how to hold the reins and where to put your other hand while you control him at a walk, jog and lope around the rail. You'll also back and reverse him.

The Usual Class Routine

- After everybody riding in the class is in the ring, walking around the rail, the judge will signal the announcer to ask for a change of gait. He'll usually ask for a trot, meaning a jog. Judges use standard signals for what they want, so you may be able to see what's coming up next. If you do see what's coming up, you can mentally prepare yourself. However, do *not* ask Primo to do it until the announcer makes it official. An obvious exception is if the judge speaks directly to you. If you know what's coming up, check on Primo's position in the arena. If you know you'll be asked to lope, for example, look for the best spot to ask Primo to start off. A finished horse should be able to take either lead and stay straight, but some horses tend to turn into the lead. If Primo does this with you, start his lope at a corner in class, so it won't be as obvious. (But work on his leads later. Read Chapters 5 and 6 for help.) If he's good about taking the proper lead on a straight line, show off this ability and hope the judge is watching. If one or more horses get too close, avoid trouble. Move to a less crowded spot. But don't change gait or direction.

- Primo will be asked to do all three gaits in both directions around the ring. To reverse, turn him to the inside. (Turn away from the rail, not toward it.) If he can do a nice turn on the haunches or foreleg, show this. Otherwise, just make a simple half-circle reverse. He'll be asked to reverse at the walk and the jog, but not at the lope.

- After a while, the judge will ask for the entries to line up. When you hear that announced, head for the center of the ring. (If Primo's been to a lot of shows, he may head for the center when he hears "Line up" without waiting for your signal. If this happens, don't correct him. Make it seem like that was your idea.) Don't rush in, but don't take too long. Find an open spot and fill it. Line up side by side. If, during rail work, you saw that Primo and another horse didn't seem to like each other, or they liked each other *too* much, don't line up next to that horse! Other line-up suggestions can be found in this chapter on page 77.

- Once you're in your spot, get Primo *squared up*. This means he'll stand straight, weight evenly distributed, one foot in each corner of an imaginary square (actually a rectangle), head pointed forward, ears alert and neck in a relaxed position. He should do this with a minimum of moves by you. (For help with squaring up, see page 84 in this chapter and page 237 in Chapter 10.)

- Be in your best normal seat position. Sit relaxed and tall, and look straight over Primo's ears. Viewed from the side, an imaginary vertical line will pass through your ear, shoulder, hip and heel.

  Your stirrups should be long for Western Pleasure,

but not so long that they don't help you. They should bear some weight. To check for length, take both feet out so your legs hang naturally. Each stirrup's base should touch your ankle bone or be just below it.

Your rein hand should have a good soft grip on the reins, with your thumb on top. Keep your wrist straight but relaxed. It shouldn't be too stiff or too limp. Let your elbow bend and stay close to your body. This is the way it should be when you ride, too. The reason for this bend is so you can open and close your elbow to follow Primo's movements. Hold your "off" hand to match the position of your rein hand, or place it in a relaxed manner on your thigh. If using romal reins, hold the romal in your off hand. (*Note*: When referring to reins and hands, the hand carrying the reins one-handed is your "near" hand. Right or left, the other is your "off" hand.)

- The judge will go to each entry down the line and ask the rider to back the horse, then return to the line. When it's your turn, just do as the judge asks.
- Depending on the size of the class and the talent of the competitors, the judge may need to see some things done more than once. Or he may ask for an extended gait. He may even have some entries stay in the lineup while he watches others work some more. If it's a large class, he might want a closer look at some horses before making a final decision.

  If this happens to you and Primo, and you're not one of the chosen ones, don't give up or change your riding position. Sometimes the top two or three winners are easy to pick, while the rest of the finalists require a second or even a third look before placing.
- The judge gives individual instructions. The

Good Western Pleasure Lope

Pal lands on his near (left) forefoot in order to do the "pull" part of the lope. His neck is stretched as far as it will go for loping at this speed. Even so, Pal's topline passes new AQHA rules against a horse with his head too low.

Lope With Head Too Low

To get this picture of Sarah's horse carrying his head too low, so you could see how it looks, we needed to make him concentrate very hard. So I asked Sarah to have Arizona countercanter in a circle around the photographer. The tips of Arizona's ears are lower than the points of his withers.

announcer's instructions usually apply to the entire class.

- It is Primo that is being judged in Western Pleasure, and his rules are clearly stated in the book. But you can help him by riding better. Study equitation in Chapter 5 and review the AHSA Chart on Stock Seat Equitation in the Appendix.

English Pleasure

You might enjoy showing Primo in Hunter Under Saddle. This English class is now in many shows that are primarily Western. Its rules are explained in the same book (for example, AQHA or APHA). Gaits include the medium walk, ordinary trot, extended trot, canter and hand gallop. (It's a "flat" class. There's no jumping). The general class routine resembles Western Pleasure. Primo remains relaxed and alert, but he is more stretched out in his way of moving.

Think of how Primo moves. In order to speed up his gaits, Primo doesn't move his legs more times to get from point A to point B. He doesn't lift his feet any higher, either. He just puts more effort into his pushes and pulls. (At least that's the way it *should* happen.)

Think of how you ride. As you sit lightly, let your body and legs adjust to the way a forward-seat saddle naturally aligns you. Don't fight the difference. Go with it. Rather than "standing" in the saddle, you'll be in more of a chair position. Your legs will be guided into stirrups that are more forward than those of most stock-seat saddles. The angle of the seat will make you want to roll a bit forward.

For flat riding, the stirrups should allow you to keep a slight bend in your knees. If the stirrups are too short, you'll come too high and/or too far forward when you're posting up. If they're too long, you'll have the same problem as with a stock-seat saddle, meaning your heels will come up when you put weight in the stirrups. Before you mount, adjust the stirrup leathers to match your arms' length. Place your fingertips where the leather attaches to the saddle. Straighten your arm. The stirrup iron should touch your armpit. Some riders tend to keep their lower legs several inches away from the horse's sides for Western riding. Let your legs fall closer to Primo's sides for English riding. This puts your legs where they're convenient to cue Primo. Also, it's easier to balance by flexing your ankles when your weight flows straight down into your stirrups. Rest the balls of your feet on the stirrup irons. If your feet are in too deep, you won't be able to flex your ankles.

The weight-bearing axis (meaning center line) for a three-point forward seat varies. Usually a boy's will be midpoint on his seatbones and a girl's will be more to the front. In either case, the axis connects his/her two hip sockets. (See the diagrams of the pelvis in Chapter 2.) This is how you'll sit when Primo stands or moves at a collected gait.

For a faster trot, you should roll and lean forward so that your CB/weight matches Primo's CB/weight and your crotch touches the saddle. In order to protect your crotch, you'll naturally brace your thighs against the saddle. When you do, you'll feel your knees contact the padded wedges in the flaps (fenders). These knee rolls help hold your two-point position. Support your weight with your legs, just above the knees, and your feet. Your calves are for cueing Primo, not to squeeze him for hanging on. Don't squeeze with your knees, either. Your knees are just stabilizers.

Keep the two-point position for a canter and a hand gallop. Primo's CB/weight shifts forward for these gaits, so your two-point position keeps your CB/weight aligned with his. (*Straddle*, don't sit on the saddle. *Sitting* makes a *three*-point position.) Good flexible ankles will support your weight as your feet bear down on the stirrups. You'll also contact the saddle with the area just above your knees. Don't squeeze. You'll feel the saddle rise and meet your crotch during the "across" part of "push-across-pull."

A good exercise for developing two-point balance is to have someone lunge Primo in a circle while you ride him without a bridle. Practice posting a trot and straddling a canter two-point. (This exercise also teaches you *not* to use the rein for balance.) The lunge rope should be at least 15 feet long, making the circle 25 to 30 feet across to avoid straining Primo's legs. Six circles in the same direction are plenty without slowing to a walk or changing directions. (This lets Primo's legs rest and helps prevent boredom.) Ride in both directions for a total of no longer than fifteen minutes. Be patient. It takes lots of practice to develop the feel and timing of keeping a two-point balance, so don't wear out your horse while you learn how to do it.

Hand gallops need even larger circles. Use a bridle, not a lunge line, so you can control his faster speeds.

Sit in the saddle to slow or stop Primo, using the same position and cues as you would for Western riding.

For a mental picture of how to be from your waist up, think of sitting straight, level and balanced. Combine this with just a hint of how you'd be if you leaned down from Primo's bare back and hugged him around the neck. It's a look of quiet strength and control that's not stiff.

Keep your elbows down near or against your sides. Keep your hands near Primo's neck (and each other) for English two-handed reining. If you stretch out your fingers, they should be able to touch Primo's neck. And if you stretch out

Lined Up Western

Teresa sits very well. Her outfit and Pal's tack look good, and the reins—held one-handed—are even and in the in-neutral position you'll learn about in Chapter 4. Pal is well groomed and wears a lovely expression. So what's wrong? Look at Pal's feet. You can see all four of them. Viewed from the side, you should only see the front and back legs/feet on one side. Pal has not been squared up, and I asked Teresa not to for the purpose of this picture.

your thumbs, they should touch an area roughly 3 inches down Primo's neck from the crest. Your hands need to move to keep up with Primo's motion, but they shouldn't move out to the side of his neck for English pleasure.

This is because you'll mainly use a direct rein, and you'll have very little slack (2 to 3 inches) while moving. Use your direct rein on either side for turns. Use them together for

Lined Up English

Miss Kitty is squared up fairly well, but her hind feet are not quite even. Also, her mane is trimmed a couple of inches below the ear, which is a style that's more Western than English. Otherwise, both rider and horse are groomed and attired for hunt seat. They look pretty good except for uneven reins. This would count more against you in an equitation class than in an English or Western pleasure class. However, Teresa is using the left rein to bring Miss Kitty's attention back to *her* instead of whatever caused the mare to appear so alert. The stirrups should be about one notch longer for pleasure. Teresa has them set for jumping. (The straps on the protective leg wraps that Miss Kitty wears for jumping should be tucked more neatly for show.)

stopping and backing. You might use an indirect rein to keep Primo positioned properly on the rail. If, for this class, you do use an open rein, keep it close to the neck.

The only time you'll have slack in the reins is during

lineup. Then Primo stands on a "free rein." Free rein is also what you use while lined up for a Western class.

Jumping

Primo might be asked to jump a low obstacle in a trail class since he might encounter a log or something similar while rounding up stock or riding out in the open. Or you might decide to show him in hunter classes with jumps. While we're thinking English, I'll explain some basics for low jumping (under 2.5 feet) in this otherwise-Western book. Read the section on crossovers in Chapter 4 before you try jumping. Apply what you learn there to here.

First of all, you'll need to shorten your stirrups, probably a couple of holes, so that your seat can stay off the saddle while Primo jumps.

- Line up Primo so that he is headed straight toward the middle of the obstacle to be jumped. Use your leg and rein to keep him from turning and "running out" at either side or from stopping (balking). Focus on the part of the obstacle (the center) that he'll clear by jumping. Think positive.
- Be in a two-point straddle position. Depending on Primo's speed, you'll either already be in this position or you'll assume it before he lifts off. As he jumps, you'll be aware of the saddle coming up to meet your crotch. It should barely miss or lightly brush your crotch. A bump means you aren't straddling high enough. Don't straddle too high, however, and don't stick your rear end up, either.
- Until you get the feel for knowing when to ask Primo to lift off, let him decide when to jump. You'll feel him

raise his front end. As his neck comes up, pla
hands on either side of his neck, wherever the
comfortable. This gives you something to brace ag
for extra security and to keep your balance without
interrupting Primo's job. For low jumps, the best spot
for your hands will be about 6 inches in front of his
withers. Don't shorten the reins. Grip them at this
length between thumb and first finger—wherever it
feels most secure without straining your hand—as
you lay your palms on Primo's neck. This position
keeps you from jerking the bit (jabbing) when Primo
stretches his neck, which he must do in order to
throw his weight forward over the jump. By bracing
yourself (flexibly, not rigidly) in this manner, you'll
naturally follow Primo's motion and automatically
match your CB with his. And the reins will be the
proper length for you to resume control after he lands.

- Primo will stretch his neck even more as he lands.
  That's when you'll let your hands follow his forward
  action. You shouldn't need to break contact with his
  neck by lifting your hands if you're jumping low
  obstacles. Just transfer weight from your palms onto
  your fingers—meanwhile continuing to grip the
  rein—and flex your wrists. (If it's difficult to carry
  your weight on fingers in a spread position, curl them
  and carry weight on your knuckles. You'll probably
  instinctively do this.)

- When Primo's back legs land, his CB/weight returns to
  a less forward position. So should yours. This is also
  when you'll resume control of the rein. If he's trotting
  from one fence (or other obstacle) to the next, resume
  posting. Otherwise, adjust your position to agree with
  the gait and speed you want Primo to take.

You'll soon work out a system with Primo on when to stay seated and when to take a two-point position. There is no firm rule here. It depends on whether Primo wants to rush at the jump or has to be driven to it. Don't let him go any faster than you can control. If he tries to rush the fence, turn him before he reaches the takeoff point. Circle him, then do something else until he's calmed down before you try any more jumping. Maybe you're afraid. If you are, Primo will know it and the situation will get worse. Jumping is fun and exciting. However, don't try it until you can control your fear. You must feel good about what you're doing for Primo to have confidence in you. If you instantly love jumping, control your enthusiasm. While learning, it's best to trot to a fence and canter a stride or two after landing. And always wear a safety helmet!

One last precaution: *Know what's on the other side of the obstacle before you jump it*. Schooling a set-up course presents no surprises (other than what Primo might decide to give). Popping over a fallen tree trunk found while riding in the woods could be a lot of fun, particularly if it's no higher than obstacles you and Primo school over. But always check the other side before you jump. Otherwise—when it's too late to avoid it—you might encounter something nasty, such as broken glass, a jagged tree stump or a hole.

Videotape Your Show Ride

If you can get someone to shoot a video of your entire show ride, including other riders for comparison, it will be a great learning tool. Ideally, this video will catch all transitions, too. (You will find information about gait transitions in Chapter 5 and lead changes in Chapter 6.) You'll discover something new each time you see the video. If you can, watch your show videos with an expert horseman. Ask what he or she thinks about the following:

- Primo's gaits, his transitions, his acceptance of your cues and his overall appearance. This includes his topline and head position as well as details of grooming and tack.
- Your control over Primo and your overall appearance. Appearance details include your body and head position, hands, legs, facial expression, personal grooming and what you wear.
- Other horses and riders appearing in the video.
- Improving your ring strategy, for example, how to position Primo in relation to other horses (whether to put him next to lighter, darker, larger or smaller horses) to show him off best, especially for lineups. The expert might point out permanent signs, posts or gates that you could use as markers during future shows at that site. If you know what to expect (as permanent markers) in the ring where you'll be showing, you can plan some of your strategy ahead of time and be prepared to concentrate more on your ride.

Perhaps the video shows you are slightly off balance when you ride. It may be that you have one leg longer than the other. To find out if that's your problem, lie down and have someone measure you from hip bone to mid-knee, then from mid-knee to ankle. A slight difference shouldn't create a problem. But if the difference is half an inch or more, you'll need to adjust your stirrups and probably make new holes. This will allow you to center yourself better by placing your weight evenly in both stirrups. It'll be easier for Primo to adjust to cues coming from two different stirrup lengths than for him to live with the problems created by a lopsided rider. It's tough on a horse to carry a rider's uneven weight and forever feel uneven seatbones.

Schooling

Now that you have an idea of what to expect at shows in general and pleasure classes in particular, let's see what goes on between you and Primo to earn that WTB look.

Just because Primo is a finished performance horse and may even have a long history of wins, it doesn't mean he'll keep doing what he was trained to do. He'll always need fine-tuning, especially for competition. More important, he needs to be tuned to "sound" right when *you* "play" him.

The Sensitive Horse

Don't be hard-handed, but don't let this clever horse get away with misbehaving. Be his boss on the ground and in the saddle. He'll probably test you with little annoying tricks, such as not standing still or playing hard to catch. If he gets away with that, he'll try bigger things, such as drifting off pattern or not responding to your signals. Be consistent and make your signals clear. Learn the important difference between making your signals *clear* and overdoing how you ask them. Be fair, but don't be afraid of hurting your horse's feelings. Don't change the rules by letting him do something sometimes but not always. If, for example, you don't want him to drop his head and graze whenever he feels like it when you're in the saddle, use a special, clear signal (such as extra rein slack *and* a pat on the neck) to allow grazing.

Try to keep the high-strung horse calm. After you saddle and mount, spend a while just standing around before you start his warm-up. (But don't stand in the way of other riders.) Quietly lean forward and stroke his neck. Lean back and rub his hindquarters, also. Keep the reins as slack as you can without losing control. If he starts to move, try using your legs, weight and "Whoa" rather than the reins to stop him. You might want to teach him the "in-neutral" halt described in Chapter 4. Whatever you do to keep your horse stopped, he must not move until you ask him to move.

On the other hand, don't invite trouble. Don't make Primo stand unreasonably long, particularly under difficult conditions (such as being attacked by insects). If you sense that he's getting restless and you've already made your point by having him stand still for a while (sometimes half a minute is long enough), ask him to move along. Always make it *your* idea, not Primo's. This keeps you in control without starting a fight.

Primo might only be nervous sometimes. When he has a nervous day, don't start a fight. Keep your workout simple. Moving from one gait to another tends to cause a high-strung horse to get tense and perhaps blow up. Jog and lope some nice easy circles in the arena, then take him out for a nice long walk along a road (without much traffic).

As a rule, a high-strung horse is smarter than average. He gets bored easily, especially by going around and around in the arena. A bored or sour horse can be a real behavior problem! Two solutions to his boredom are (1) changing the usual routine and (2) presenting a challenge. You'll find several suggestions in this book as well as in *Ride Western Style*.

Sometimes a horse acts high strung because he lacks self-confidence and/or lacks confidence in his rider. This is not a good horse for you because he's the type that can blow up when he gets upset. Rarely will his type be a good performance horse, and the exceptional, talented one needs an experienced rider to maintain his confidence.

The Lazy Performance Horse

A lazy Primo might be hiding some championship talent. Your challenge is to convince him to unpack and use it! This requires keeping your signals consistent and showing authority. A lazy horse can also be quite clever. You must first call his bluff in order to win his respect. Practicing extended gaits is particularly good for developing impulse within the lazy horse. However, you'll probably need a lot of leg to drive him until he realizes that you expect a certain amount of energy on his part, too. Then ease back until you feel him start to get lazy again.

Sitting in the saddle, you'll drive Primo by working your seatbones in a motion similar to walking. Move them back and forth in rhythm with his motion. As Primo's back leg stretches forward, it rolls his barrel to the opposite side. As his barrel comes up under your leg, it sends your leg forward. When you feel your leg go forward, emphasize your rolling motion by pushing with your seatbone.

For riding in a two-point position, drive with your inner thighs. Again, take advantage of the natural motion. (As you'll later learn, a two-point position is not limited to English riding or faster gaits.)

Bad Habits and Other Problems

If Primo dances and jigs when you ask him to walk and jog, first you need to find out why he won't settle down. Is it a habit he already had? If so, you can't expect to change him overnight. But most bad habits can be broken.

As soon as you feel Primo start to stiffen and speed up, for example, don't tighten or grip more with your legs or hands. Instead, make a big effort to relax yourself. Sometimes that's all it takes to get him to relax and behave.

If relaxing doesn't work, don't waste time letting Primo misbehave. Disobedience cannot be allowed. To cure Primo's bad habit (or to keep misbehavior from becoming a habit), you must be able to feel or see the problem early. You must react before he really gets a chance to get away with whatever it is. (If you're riding him, maybe you'll feel his body get hard or maybe he'll pin his ears back or toss his head.) Once you notice the problem, be consistent in how you respond to it. Discourage his wrong move by turning it into something unpleasant.

For example, use a series of short firm tugs with the reins to back or circle Primo. (Of course, you don't want Primo to associate being backed and circled with being disciplined. To keep from confusing him, *keep your legs off* when you're disciplining him with the reins. And be more gentle with the reins when you're using them as an aid.)

Sooner or later Primo will do what you originally asked without a fight, because it's easier than what he'd tried doing that was wrong. It's definitely more pleasant than what he found himself doing next. And he's convinced that this thing he's doing for you now was *his* idea.

This way of thinking in harmony with your horse is what Ray Hunt teaches in his book, *Think Harmony with Horses*, and in clinics all over the world. It's a wonderful method, and Ray's expressions are very colorful and clear. For example:

- "Make the wrong things difficult, and the right things easy."
- "Let your idea become the horse's idea."
- "Your horse is not your slave—he's your partner."

However, as this modern horsemaster readily admits, his general philosophy is not original. There have been other great horsemasters throughout history. Many of today's best training and riding methods are based on the writings of Xenophon, a Greek cavalry officer who lived around 400 B.C.

Good Riding Tips

This information applies to all kinds of riding. However, it especially fits Western pleasure competition:

- Practice riding without stirrups. I promise you'll love it. Don't be surprised if you feel Primo relax as soon as you let your feet hang free. This happens because *you* are more relaxed. You should be able to feel an immediate difference, from top to bottom. Riding without stirrups is a great way to deepen your seat, to improve your legs and overall balance. It provides the many advantages of riding bareback along with the safety of a saddle.
- Primo's gaits should be clean, not sloppy. He should have four distinct beats to his walk, two beats to his jog and three to his lope. Obviously, this cannot be determined unless the ground is good. As you learned in Chapter 1, if the surface is too deep, uneven, slick or otherwise tricky, Primo's gait will be affected. Otherwise, any gait change from what's described in

Chapter 2 means that Primo is being sloppy, is lame or needs reshoeing.

- Most gait sloppiness is caused by bad riding. Perhaps the rider has too much contact on the reins or doesn't use enough leg to drive the horse. Closer rein contact is the wrong approach for some horses. Usually, a horse who wants a looser rein will toss his head. If Primo doesn't stay level and smooth (to "flow low to the ground") or tosses his head, try giving him more rein slack. ("Throw the reins away.") Use more leg and seatbones to drive him.

- On the other hand, some horses really round their backs while loping. If you sit deep for their lope, it'll feel like a lot of smooth little leaps or bucks. If this is Primo's way, you may need to lighten your seatbones for his lope. To do this, step harder into your stirrups. Some horses will refuse to take a proper lead for loping if they are squeezed or if they are driven too hard by the seatbone cue. They likewise do better with more weight in the stirrups.

- Keep Primo interested *and* paying attention to you. It's okay for him to look around a bit when he first comes into the ring. That gives him a nice, alert expression. Still, don't let him take advantage of it. As everybody files around the ring the first time, test Primo's attention by lifting your rein hand, then returning it. This is called "bumping." Bump him every few strides. If you don't see his ear turn slightly back in a "I hear you" response, then bump a stronger "Hey, remember me?" contact.

  You might need to lift the reins 5 or 6 inches as the punishment part of a bump, then release them to reward Primo when he does what you ask. You might need to move them no more than an inch. You might need to bump at each stride for about three strides, or do it only once. This can vary from horse to horse and even from time to time with the same horse. Move the reins just enough to get Primo to respond.

You'll find other uses for bumping. For example, you can use it before asking for a gait or lead change. Bumping can remind Primo to round his back or lower his head, too. Just don't overuse this tool, or Primo will tune it out.

• One way to keep Primo tuned to respond to a flick of your wrist on the slack rein required in Western Pleasure competition is to school him on a shorter rein. This means just an inch or two of slack, as for English riding. Of course, your hand must follow Primo's head movement so you don't accidentally jab him. Otherwise, slack is slack. He doesn't know whether it's 2 inches or 2 feet. He'll feel the rein slide on his neck. And then he'll contact the bit.

• *Always* reward your horse promptly after he's done what you want him to do. Try not to lose your patience or your temper. And *never* give a "peace offering" reward when he's not even trying to do what you ask. A reward helps Primo realize he's done what you expect. If you give it to him anyway, right or wrong, how is he supposed to learn what you really want? The only way you can reward him during a show is to relax the pressure from your cues. When you're not in the show ring, however, you can praise him by pats, hugs or kind words. This reward makes you both feel good.

• If you plan on showing Primo primarily in pleasure

class, you shouldn't practice faster than a lope in the arena. Save the faster gaits for rides outside of the arena. Besides, if you *do* show Primo in reining and other classes with speedy patterns, you won't be asked to gallop him next to the rail. That's one reason why these classes, including barrel racing, keep speed work away from the rail.

- Practice most of your loping alone. Horses will instinctively want to race if they're loping side by side. You don't want to encourage racing.
- However, it's a good idea to keep Primo used to sharing the arena with other ridden horses. In the ring, sometimes another horse will stop abruptly in front of you and Primo, or appear out of nowhere and cut you off.

So you'll how to handle such problems during a class, get another rider to do these things purposely during practice. Usually you can get out of the way and keep going forward by using your leg to move Primo over laterally. Sometimes you might need to slow down to avoid a wreck, but try to avoid stopping completely. If a close call happens during a lope, be sure Primo is on the proper lead before you continue. Depending on how Primo acts after the problem, you'll need to (1) relax yourself to relax him, (2) bump the reins to get his attention again, (3) drive him more with your legs, (4) a combination of the above or (5) keep going as though it never happened because evidently that's the way Primo is treating it.

Roadwork

Roadwork is not limited to schooling Primo. It's equally useful for schooling his rider. Use roadwork as a chance to practice keeping yourself lined up properly without being stiff. Remember to look ahead, not down at Primo's shoulder or the ground. A quick peek down is okay. Remember to breath properly, too. And practice wearing a pleasant expression. Even when a rider's having a great time, he or she will frown from concentrating hard.

Find a place to ride that has little traffic, few turns and good footing for putting some miles on Primo. It could be a quiet road, a bridle path or a big pasture. This is where you can improve Primo's impulse and build his stamina by doing the extended walk and trot. (It's a good workout for you, too.) Just don't trot fast on hard ground.

After you've pushed Primo up to the extended gait, keep him at it awhile, then gradually slow him until he's doing the same gait at the proper show speed. Keep him at this speed for a longer while. Let him know he's doing a really good job at it before asking him for any changes.

The easiest time to get a good extended walk is on the way home. This applies to both a sensitive horse and a lazy one. Just don't do anything faster than an extended walk. Don't jog, although it's actually slower. You're always supposed to walk Primo back to the barn. But in the real world, sometimes emergencies require you to hurry home. If so, be sure Primo gets cooled out and cared for promptly.

Warm-Up

A warm-up is very important for both horse and rider. It prepares mind and body for a performance. That performance can be a regular workout or it can be a competition event. You and Primo will last much longer as a riding team with a good warm-up before the ride and a good cool-down afterwards. You *each* need this routine.

Certainly no horse should be expected to go into a show ring and do his best without a proper warm-up. Once you've determined whether Primo is a high-strung, super-responsive horse or more inclined to be lazy, you will be better able to prepare him for a show class. A rule of thumb is, if it takes ten minutes at home to get Primo warmed up and ready to work, it will take fifteen to twenty minutes at a show. The extra time allows both of you to get used to the ground conditions and excitement from being in a new place with other performers.

If Primo's too wound up to do well in pleasure class, take him to an uncrowded area and ride him down a bit. Don't wear him out, however.

If he's somewhat asleep, take him to an uncrowded area and ride him through more transitions than you would if he were nervous. Warm-ups take less time for a lazy horse. You just want to wake him up and get him past being sloppy. If he knows how to do lateral work, this practice will help him. Keep him fresh so that when he enters the ring, he'll be alert and interested, not dull or sour.

Schooling Shows

At first, all of your shows will be schooling shows. Even if Primo's a seasoned campaigner, you are not. Depending on where you live, however, you just may find yourself sharing the same ring with some world-class riders. This happens more often at "breed shows" (such as AQHA- or APHA-sponsored shows). The reason is a trainer will use a relatively low-key local show that you're part of as a schooling show for a young horse (or rider) prior to the big league. Just as you improve with experience, so does the student he or she is training.

Even though you're never supposed to school during a show class, occasionally a big-name trainer will rough up a horse to "teach it a lesson" after the horse gets disqualified. Not *all* noted trainers are guilty of taking advantage of schooling shows. In fact, most will keep a low profile at them and are courteous and eager to help a new generation of performers.

For the most part, schooling shows are great. They build confidence (whether you win anything or not) and give you valuable experience without a lot of pressure. Judges are generally willing to explain more to entrants than they can under more formal conditions at prestigious shows.

What You and Primo Wear

Your clothes and Primo's tack are also judged. His equipment should fit, be clean and be in good repair. Details make a difference. Be sure that the pad and blanket are matched and even under the saddle and that all the straps are secured.

A winning outfit helps present your WTB look. It can help you look straighter, more balanced, taller or slimmer. A winning outfit can also cost a fortune. But it doesn't have to. The trick is to spend your money where it does the most good.

Your hat is your crowning glory. Start with a top-quality hat in a neutral color. Neutral colors (gray tones, black or beige tones) can look casual or elegant. Buy the highest-quality beaver hat you can afford. Hat makers grade their felt fur hats with an "X" rating. The higher the number, the higher the quality of fur (beaver). Experts recommend a 10X or above for the show ring. Lower numbers mean the beaver fur is blended with rabbit hair or wool. After you buy the hat, get it blocked and creased by an expert. He'll crease the hat to suit your face and build.

Headwear is seasonal. Felt (beaver) is worn in fall and winter. Straw is worn from April through September.

After you get your hat, take good care of it. Since the better-quality hat uses more naturally water-resistant fur, a fine beaver hat can tolerate rain or snow better than a cheaper felt hat. If it gets wet, just shake off the excess water and let it dry naturally. And keep it brushed.

The best place for your hat is on your head. (Put it on front-to-back by holding the brim, not the crown.) To store your hat, put in a box, *crown* side down. (In other words, store your hat upside down.)

Speaking of hats, I'd like to put in a good word for Western safety helmets. They are not as stylish as a Stetson or Resistol, but they come close enough if you consider and value protection for your head.

Next on the list are chaps. You can save money if you find a used pair that can be altered to fit. Be sure to save any scraps from altering or making your chaps. Use the scraps to trim your vest or shirts, or for making covered buttons for your jacket. Chaps don't have to match your hat as long as the hat is a complementary neutral color. Men can always wear indigo blue jeans, but women and youths must match their pants to their chaps. For that reason, select a color that will be easy to match with off-the-rack pants. The color should also look good next to Primo. (Black is hard to beat.) Chaps should be long enough to cover all but the toe of your boot when you're in the saddle. (They're supposed to drag on the ground when you walk; you're supposed to turn up the cuffs.) Chaps can be Ultrasuede or leather. Ultrasuede comes in a variety of colors and is machine washable. Leather costs less and makes a better fringe.

Next come boots. Ropers come in many colors. You might consider getting a pair to match your saddle, so your foot will blend with your stirrup.

You'll need a pair of Western dress pants for halter or showmanship. The fabric in dress pants might be delicate, so don't use them for riding. For your other events, get two or three pairs of the brand of jeans that fit you best.

Any kind of jacket will do as long as it looks good on you. If you use it for riding events, be sure it's cut to fit nicely when you sit in the saddle. A vest can add color without much cost. So can scarves. As for shirts or blouses (or sweaters, belts or gloves), be guided by your own imagination, taste and budget. When in doubt, remember: tuxedo shirts are always correct.

Here's a description of "appointments" (your clothing, Primo's tack) that satisfy AHSA, AQHA and APHA rules for stock-seat equitation and / or Western horsemanship. While it offers a nice variety, it doesn't list all the possibilities or tell what's popular where you live. Riders dress a little differently in California than in Texas, in Wisconsin than in Florida and so forth. Besides, you don't have to live in the United States to ride or show Western. Maybe you live in Canada or England. Some of you may be reading this book (and *Ride Western Style*) in German or another language. Stock-seat riding is truly gaining world-wide popularity.

Appointment rules are flexible enough to allow each rider to dress in a manner that flatters his or her figure. Dress to give an even appearance, so your upper body is in proportion to your legs. If you aren't naturally tall and slim, you can dress to fool the eye. For example, a slightly baggy shirt "shortens" someone with a very long torso. So will matching the top third of your blouse or shirt with the color of your chaps. A ruffled or bold-patterned top adds pounds. A solid-color tuxedo shirt worn with pants of a matching or blending color is more slimming. Read my suggestions here, visit local shows, study magazine photos of winning riders, study catalogs and then decide what's best for you.

Your clothing must be workmanlike for equitation classes. Save the vest and jacket for other show events. Wear pants and a long-sleeved shirt, or a one-piece equitation jumpsuit with shirtlike collar and cuffs. If the jumpsuit has a zipper closing, it must be covered with a fold of fabric that has buttons or snaps attached (like a regular shirt front).

Your clothes must fit properly. Pants and shirt should not be too long, too short, too tight or too baggy. You're required to wear a belt under loops, boots and a Western hat. (A safety helmet is optional.) You also must wear a necktie, kerchief or bolo tie. Chaps are required for AHSA but optional for AQHA and APHA. Spurs are optional, period. For all shows, your hair must be neat and securely fastened if it's long enough to cover your number. The rules don't mention jewelry, but I will. Rings and bracelets can do more than distract Primo or you. They can be dangerous. They can get tangled in reins and / or mane.

Primo's saddle must fit you. The shape of the fork or cantle doesn't matter. The seat's size does. A narrow seat is usually more comfortable for youngsters and women. (But be sure the tree is wide enough for Primo.) A saddle with a steep rise to the seat tends to roll you back too far. A slight rise helps you keep a good seat. Also, AHSA rules state that nothing can be added or removed to keep the stirrups from hanging freely. (This guards against somebody rigging the stirrups so they won't move even if the rider's uncontrolled legs "want" to swing them.) Tapaderos (stirrup hoods) are optional for AQHA horsemanship classes. They're not even mentioned in APHA or AHSA rules.

Any standard Western bit is allowed. This means a curb bit that has a solid or broken mouthpiece, has shanks and acts with leverage. For AHSA stock-seat equitation, the judge must have the bits dropped and inspected on all finalists. All rules require curb chains or straps to be at least ½ inch wide. No wire, metal or rawhide device is allowed. Hackamores, tie-downs of any kind, running martingales or draw reins are not permitted either. AHSA and APHA only allow bits and one-handed reining. AQHA allows snaffles and bosals on horses four years old or younger, using standard two-handed reining rules. For AHSA, if closed (romal) reins are used, hobbles must be carried attached below the cantle or on the near side of the saddle. Hobbles are optional for AQHA and APHA. The rules all say that if split reins are used, no hobbles are necessary. A rope lariat (reata) must be carried attached to the fork of the saddle for AHSA but is optional for AQHA and APHA. All rules allow silver equipment, but silver shall not be given preference over good working equipment.

Only standard shoes are allowed on Primo's back feet for AHSA. The iron that forms the shoe can be no wider than 1 inch. (This eliminates some versions of "slider plates.") AQHA and APHA simply require the shoes to be safe and securely fitted to the horse's feet.

A judge will let Primo wear leg protection if he's been injured. In most cases, he can also wear leg protection in competition whose tests require spins, rollbacks and / or sliding stops. However, some classes do not allow boots or leg wraps. Check your rule books well ahead of show time.

Primo himself must also be shiny and sleek. Several good books on grooming are listed in the Appendix.

Squaring Up Under Saddle

Stop Primo where you want him to line up. (You'll learn how to put the reins down for an "in neutral" stop in Chapter 4. This stop should keep Primo from moving in response to your moving to check on his feet.) Use as little motion as possible to lean down and check on his feet. If you're lucky, he'll already be squared up. He'll have one foot in each corner of a rectangle in a way that sets him up best for his conformation. You might want to ask an expert for help on deciding what's best for Primo. Most Western-type horses look best with their legs set in a natural position, not stretched out like a gaited horse.

If his hind feet are even, leave them alone. If one is too far back, you'll need to get it more under him. This is easier to do by backing. Put a little extra weight on your seatbone *on whichever side the hind foot is too far back.* Let's say it's his right hind foot. You'd shift to your right, ask Primo for one step straight back, and then halt. This should put his right hind foot where it's even with his left hind foot. If it doesn't come out that way, calmly ask him to step forward a step or two, stop him, then check his hind feet. Maybe they'll be even this time. If not, back him again, shifting your weight to whichever foot is farther back. Repeat going forward and back until his hind feet are even.

Next check on his front feet. Maybe they're already even.

If not, use your toe to nudge the elbow of whichever leg needs to move up. Keep it easy and calm. If Primo ends up with his front feet out too far, you'll have to start all over. Begin with his hind feet and follow the same steps. As soon as Primo squares up nicely, praise him and relax.

CHAPTER 4

—◆◀●▶◆—

Trail Horse

Trail class judges Primo's performance over obstacles. The emphasis is partly on his manners and attitude while handling the obstacles, and partly on his response to your cues. Unlike pleasure class, trail class is an individual event. You and Primo have the show arena to yourselves. Trail and pleasure work well together, however. You can school Primo on trail routines to improve his pleasure performance, and vice versa, because both classes concentrate on calm obedience rather than speed and flashy action. Both performance events are safe enough for a novice rider (on a well-broke horse), but they also challenge and attract a professional rider/trainer.

Trail as a Training Tool

You'll learn, in this chapter, how to train Primo to be a trail horse. If you wonder why I tell you how to train a horse that's already supposed to be finished, here's why:

- You need to know what Primo's supposed to do before you can cue him to do it. In trail class, like pleasure class, Primo gets judged but you must work as a team. For example, Primo aligns and changes his position for going through a gate, but you have to open and shut it. The same logic applies to working a mailbox, a slicker (raincoat) and hobbles. (Hobbles are ropes designed to tie two legs and leave just enough slack for Primo to walk slowly as he grazes.)
- Even though Primo knows exactly what to do, he's not supposed to do it until you ask him. It must be clear to the judges that he's doing what you ask, when you ask it.
- For this reason, you need to develop the kind of control that has Primo responding to *you*, not to situations.
- Primo may know some, but not all of the obstacles used in trail classes. He might have forgotten some of his early training. He might have grown careless. Like all performance athletes and machines, even the best trail horses need regular tune-ups in order to do their best.

Rest and Relaxation as a Training Tool

This is a good time to point out one thing: *Don't overtrain.* If you want Primo to do his best as a performance horse, he needs free time to do nothing but be a horse. Turnout is his R & R (rest and relaxation), his safety valve for letting off steam and forgetting any anxieties. Half an hour or more of turnout each day (or night, if days are too hot or buggy) is a training tool that's as important as riding itself.

Primo's turnout area doesn't have to be a lush pasture, although that would be nice. But it must have a secure fence. It must be safe from poisonous weeds and trash that he can get hurt on. It should be big enough (at least 25 yards square) for Primo to charge around in, offer him shelter from the elements and have good footing. Fresh, clean water must always be available to him during turnout.

If the weather permits, ride Primo outside of the arena at least twice each week, for at least an hour each time. Riding with no fences is just as important as arena schooling and turnout for mental and physical conditioning.

Controlling Primo

Two-handed Control

Even though you'll compete one-handed, it's smart to start your trail work at home on Primo by reining two-handed. Usually you'll use a snaffle bit or a bosal-style hackamore. But if you already have a side-pull hackamore (it has a hard rope noseband that rolls across Primo's nose when the reins are moved, much like a bosal does), it will do quite nicely, provided it's adjusted to fit him. By whichever headpiece or mouthpiece you use, two reins let you ask more clearly for important lateral (sideways) moves.

A good way to understand how a snaffle rein works is to hold the bit in your hand and feel it move. Ask a friend to move the reins like you would for cues. Experiment with all kinds of signals. Primo's mouth will feel what your hand feels as it holds the bit that's being moved by the reins.

A bosal hackamore lets you control Primo two-handed without the risk of hurting his mouth. When you pull back on the reins, the bosal puts pressure on the flexible lower portion of Primo's nasal bone. It also rubs around the outside of his lips and squeezes his jawbones. Depending on how it's used, this causes him to flex at the poll, to stop or to turn. When you use a leading (opening) rein, Primo responds to the pull of the rein and the bosal's pressure on the opposite side of his lips and jawbones.

Special "Picture" Expressions

Penny Gibbs is noted for producing great trail horses. I've learned a great deal from reading her articles on training the trail horse in *Performance Horseman* magazine. You're familiar with my special expressions, like think-talk and WTB. Penny also uses special expressions. Three of her terms paint such a clear picture that I'll explain them here and use them hereafter.

- *In neutral* is Penny's term for ceasing all movement. Using her method, we'll teach Primo to *stop when you lower your hands to his withers.* Leave a little slack in the reins. If you need to tighten the reins and say "Whoa," do it. Tightened reins only reinforce this meaning of "stop."
- Putting Primo *in gear* is Penny's term for giving him permission to move forward. You do it by raising your reins to pommel height (about 3 inches off his neck). He'll feel this motion and be ready. You'll change the slack when asking Primo to back, turn and sidepass, but keep the reins at least 3 inches off his neck any time you want him to move.
- Penny describes a *brace rein* as "one that maintains light pressure from bit or bosal straight back to your elbow." It's basically what I describe as an indirect

rein because it's a back-up tool. But she uses it both on and off the neck, and applies it as a gentle brake.

- To understand what Penny calls *opening the door*, think of Primo as being a rectangular box with six doors. Four of those doors represent sideways motion by his legs. He has a front door and a back door on the right side and also on the left side. He also has a door in front and a door in back. Get the picture? If you imagine the box as being so full of energy wanting to escape that the doors are kept locked, then you know what will happen if one of those six doors gets opened. That's where his energy spills out.

Consider your natural aids (hands, legs, weight and voice, plus think-talk) as being keys to Primo's doors. The general idea is to use your keys to keep all of Primo's doors shut except for the ones you want him to move through.

Teaching the In-Neutral and In-Gear Cues

Sometimes using *tightened* reins as a stop signal will not work. For example, if you are working Primo through a back-through (a pattern done by backing) and he started to rush, you'd only encourage him to go faster if you pulled back on the reins. Saying "Whoa" or sitting deeper and bracing your legs should stop Primo. But a different reining cue, a relaxed-rein stopping cue, is good insurance. Here's how to teach him the in-neutral stopping cue and the in-gear cue to move. The methods fit together.

- If you don't already do this, start now to use voice commands even when handling Primo on the ground.

This will help him understand that "Whoa" always means "stop" and clucking always means "go."

For example, you've haltered Primo for grooming. Cluck and say "Walk" before you lead him. Reinforce with a tug on the lead line if he doesn't move right away. When you get to where you'll park him, say "Whoa" before tying him. If he makes a move in any direction (even a step), use pressure on your line to put him exactly where he was when you said "Whoa." Be very consistent with these voice commands (or whatever voice commands for stop and go that you normally use). Insist that Primo obey them. To him, moving a few inches when he's not supposed to means "See what I got away with?" as much as if he'd loped off to the next county!

- Read Primo's body language. A shift in weight, perked-up ears or a restless snort can warn you that he's planning to move. This is the best time to remind him to stay stopped. But match your signals to his. If his language signals are mild, keep your "Whoa" soft. This applies to all cues. Save the severe ones for when they're really needed. And use think-talk.

- Apply the same principles when you mount Primo. Say (and think) "Whoa," using pressure on the reins if he moves. If he does move, step down and put him back in his original position. Then start over. Do this as often as you have to, *taking care not to lose your temper*, until Primo stands motionless until asked to move.

- When you're ready to go, hold your reins at pommel height (about 8 inches apart, using two reins) with 2 to 3 inches of slack. Cluck "Go" and say "Walk."

Reinforce this in-gear signal with leg pressure if he
doesn't start walking.

- Once you have Primo moving, keep your hands at the
  in-gear position. Move your hand sideways to turn
  him, and toward your chest or up to take up slack for
  backing him. But *don't lower your hands unless you want
  Primo to stop.*
- When you do want him to stop, say "Whoa" and
  immediately *drop your hands to the withers* to put him
  on a relaxed rein. If Primo connects this word and
  action to the neutral-gear method of stopping and he
  halts right away, terrific! Just don't praise him so hard
  that you startle him into moving again. If he doesn't
  understand yet, simply repeat "Whoa" and reinforce
  it with light rearward pressure on the reins. Another
  reinforcement cue is to lower your ring fingers and
  gently poke Primo's neck, saying "whoa." Drop your
  hands to his withers the *instant* Primo comes to a halt.
  Then keep your hands lowered for a few moments
  and let him stand. If he tries to move, pull-release
  with the reins and say "Whoa" again.
- As soon as Primo "says" that he understands the new
  neutral-gear signal for stopping, move him along. Use
  the in-gear signal for this. Be consistent in using these
  cues on Primo if you want consistent responses from
  him.

Maybe these questions are on your mind: "How can I train
Primo to use this neutral-gear signal to stop him for trail
work and get him to stay motionless for lineup in a pleasure
class? Won't I lose points if I hold the reins down on his
neck?"

They are good questions. The answer is based on voice commands and think-talk. Remember, Primo has now been taught to respond to "Whoa" for stop and your cluck plus gait word for "go." After you've taught him to stop by the neutral-gear signal two-handed, you'll make minor adjustments so that he'll understand it for one-handed reining. From that point on, you should only need to say "Whoa" and use stop cues with your legs and weight. Whether you drop the reins or not, he should stop. If he doesn't, pull the reins back.

If Primo tries to move before you put him in gear, reinforce your "Whoa" voice cue with another pulled-back rein cue for stopping. Otherwise, everything's the same. The in-gear rein cue is good for any performance activity.

Desensitizing Primo

To desensitize Primo, you get him used to something so that it doesn't bother him. When Primo seems to understand your neutral-gear and in-gear signals, he's ready to be desensitized to the extra body motions of yours that are necessary during trail maneuvers. He needs to get used to your extra body motions and not move while you lean over to open a gate, for example. Start by putting him in neutral and placing the reins in one hand. Reach back with your free hand and try to touch his tail, then reach up and try to touch his ear. Stand up in the stirrups. Lean down and touch each stirrup.

Control for One Step Forward

Next, Primo must to learn to accept your stop and go signals when they are given much closer together than you would ask for during ordinary riding. This is so you can control his every step (in any direction) for moving through tricky patterns.

At first, you'll only deal with controlling Primo's forward motion. Use your stop and go signals until he's reached the point where he'll stop after taking only one step. Carefully mix the rapid-fire signals with some long, uninterrupted walk or jog sessions, so Primo won't start tossing his head or otherwise show his impatience.

Help him here. Keep yourself as calm as possible and your signals as light as possible. Reward all good efforts.

However, don't let Primo take advantage of you. If he disobeys, immediately discipline him. Make your discipline clear so he understands what he did wrong. Then forgive him. Don't pick on him or hold a grudge. Move right along.

Spend a little time (maybe fifteen minutes) each day on these new methods of asking Primo to stop and go. Don't overdrill, and don't introduce anything else until you're sure Primo understands what you want him to do. This will probably take a couple of weeks. Sometimes, however, it takes longer to teach a horse something, even for an expert trainer. If you feel you need outside help, get it. Don't risk losing your self-confidence or your bond with Primo.

Backing

Next, teach him the one-step control for backing.

Before backing, Primo should be straight. If he's well broke, you'll only need to "pick up" the reins (pull softly back and slightly up for rein pressure) and say "Back." If this doesn't work, shift to a slightly forward body position. Put more weight in your stirrups as you pick up the reins and say "Back." For an even stronger cue, add alternating your weight in the stirrups.

Rather than continue to use strong signals for backing Primo, teach him what the verbal command "Back" means. Otherwise, he'll just get more confused by extra cues when you get into advanced back-throughs, involving lateral work. It's easy to do from the ground. Use the same plan you used for teaching him "Whoa." This time say "Back" and push on his chest. Reward Primo for the slightest step backward. Do it every single time. He'll soon catch on.

Once he understands "Back," try eliminating leg and weight cues. When he will back from your slight pressure on the reins and saying "Back," he's ready for even finer control:

- From a halt, raise your hands from neutral to in-gear, but don't apply any rein pressure. Cluck "Go" before you say "Back."
- When he's moved a couple of steps back, drop the reins to neutral position and say "Whoa." If he tries to keep on moving back, try pushing your fingertips into his neck. Or push your seatbones down and apply leg pressure in the usual cues to stop him.
- Let him stay in neutral for a few seconds, then ask him to back again. Stop him, let him stand, then repeat.
- Gradually shorten the distance Primo backs until you can get him to move just one step back and then calmly stop. Practice daily for about a week before trying anything new.

Regardless of what you're schooling Primo for, two keys to your success are (1) endless patience and (2) thinking like a horse. Develop a sensitivity to Primo's ways of talking. When he says that he's had enough drill, end it while the situation is still under your control and do something else that's fun for you both. Otherwise you can make a lazy horse more stubbornly lazy (also clumsy) than before or turn a more sensitive horse into a nervous wreck!

Lateral Moves

Lateral moves use those side doors in Primo's "box." I'll briefly define all the lateral moves used for Western riding here, so you can compare them. Anything not explained here will be explained in Chapter 6.

A reminder: Horsemen use a variety of terms, some of which mean the same thing. In that case, your choice depends on where you live and / or where you first study riding. For example, *girth* and *cinch* mean the same thing, and Westerners usually say cinch. But I say girth (basically an English term) because I learned to ride English style before riding Western. The only riding books available to me were English. Although I ride mainly Western now, I still say girth. Some terms may have meanings different from what I describe here. If you hear someone use a term that you don't understand, don't be shy or embarrassed to ask what it means. (Ask the person who used the term. And later, ask another horseman.)

Two moves are basic to doing most lateral moves. One is a *turn on the foreleg* (or the forehand): One of Primo's front legs stays in place while he uses his hindquarters to move around it. The other is a *turn on the haunches* (or a turn over the hocks): One of Primo's back legs stays in place while he moves around it with his forelegs.

Other than for trail moves, a turn on the haunches has more uses in Western riding than a turn on the foreleg. Both moves begin with a simple crossover step—in front for a turn on the haunches, in back for a turn on the foreleg.

Here are the other circular moves. A *pivot* (or offset) is a turn on the haunches that involves making a 90-degree turn (quarter circle) or 180-degree turn (half circle) with speed. It's always performed from a halt. A *rollback* is another kind of turn on the haunches. Primo lopes or gallops from point A to point B, makes a quick 180, then lopes or gallops back to point A on the opposite lead. It's all one continuous action. A *spin* is performed as a full (360-degree) turn on the haunches. It can be done slowly or with speed. A *turnaround* uses the middle of Primo's body as his point of rotation for making a complete and careful (slow) circle. He alternates using a turn on the foreleg with a turn on the haunches. He circles by turning around a base under where you sit, not by turning around his back leg, which is in place. (*Note*: "Turnaround" is commonly used in reining to mean a spin.)

The sidepass and the two-track are straight lateral moves. In a *sidepass*, Primo's front and hind legs cross in pairs. Primo moves from point A to point B, but his motion is neither forward nor backward. It's all to one side. To *two-track*, Primo makes two parallel sets of tracks by moving on about a 45-degree angle, both forward and sideways at the same time.

Turn on the Foreleg:

I prefer saying "foreleg" to "forehand" because it makes you think of Primo turning around one leg. What I describe here goes back to basics. Neither you nor Primo may have to go through all of these steps. If not, fine. That's what you're aiming for. But it's also okay to use all of the steps to school him and for teaching yourself.

Let's ask Primo to turn around his right foreleg. This means that you want his hindquarters to move to the left and his right foreleg to stay in place. (Actually, Primo will have to lift his right foot slightly several times as he turns, but he should put it back in almost the same spot.)

- Put Primo in gear and use enough of a leading right rein to tip his head. Don't cluck or pull him around yet.
- Meanwhile, use a left brace rein and move your right leg about 8 inches behind the girth. Do not apply pressure yet. You're only getting ready.
- Now, increase pressure on the right rein, but not enough to make Primo move into turning right.
- Meanwhile, push your right seatbone down and apply pressure behind the girth with your right calf.
- At the same time, lift your left leg off. (Don't stick it way out.) Cluck and say "Over."

Think of what you've done. You've asked Primo to move, but kept his front door closed (with the help of your left brace rein). You have not invited him to move out the back door, but you have made a commotion at the *right* back side of his box. By lifting your left leg off, you've clearly opened Primo's *left* back door for escaping the commotion.

If he doesn't respond by moving his hindquarters left, then apply more pressure with your right seatbone and lower leg. (You might have to use a very light touch with your right spur to get his attention at first.)

A video of this (done correctly, of course) will show Primo crossing his right hind leg in front of his left hind leg, moving his left hind leg over and crossing it again with his right hind leg. He'll keep on doing this to move his hindquarters around. His left front foot will take little mincing steps to keep balance, and his right front foot will lift and set down just enough to keep from getting twisted. (You can also notice changes in the space between Primo's back and the backside of the saddle as his body moves around, but you only need to study what his feet and legs are doing now. If you have problems, an expert could probably make helpful suggestions based upon your video.)

Switch all sides for a turn around the left foreleg.

Turn on the Haunches: A turn on the haunches is the opposite of a turn on the foreleg. One of Primo's back legs stays in place while he moves around it with his forelegs. For a *right* turn on the haunches, which I'll now describe, Primo plants his right rear leg and his forelegs move around it to the right.

- Put Primo in gear and start with a slight direct pull on the left rein. This gets his attention and should stop his left front foot. Keep a brace on that left rein to discourage him from moving forward.
- Cluck and give a leading pull with the right rein. This starts the turn. Remember just to coax, not to pull with the leading rein. Practice will tell you how much adjustment to make with each rein. You want him to circle, not go forward or back.
- Hold the *right* back door closed by bringing your right leg back behind the girth, but don't apply pressure. This unlocks the right front door but doesn't open it yet.
- Say "Over" and push Primo through that right front door by putting *left* leg pressure just about at the girth. This automatically sets up both of your seatbones. Your right seatbone is lighter, your left seatbone will drive. If Primo doesn't move his forelegs to the right, move your foot slightly more forward. Don't move it up too far, however. *Never use spurs in front of the girth.*

A video of this will show Primo crossing his left front foot over his right, then moving his right foot over, then crossing it again with his left. His right hind foot is his pivot foot. It carries most of the weight. His left hind foot is used only for balance.

Reverse right and left for a *left* turn on the haunches.

Sidepass: Once you can get Primo to do a turn on the foreleg and a turn on the haunches, getting him to sidepass is fairly easy. Rather than doing the whole thing at once, even if Primo already knows how to sidepass, it's better for you to ask it in stages. Let's do a simple sidepass to the *right*.

- Start by having Primo in a nicely balanced halt.
- Put him in gear but keep the front door closed. Use a left direct rein braced on his neck and a right open rein braced about 3 inches off his neck. Don't cluck yet.
- Bring your left foot forward until the heel of your boot is next to the girth. Let it hang in light contact with Primo's side to keep his left back door closed.
- Take your right leg completely off his side to open *both* right side doors. So far, you've been setting him up.
- Now, do this all at the same time: (1) Cluck and say "Over," (2) press your left calf firmly against the girth (or whatever spot in that area works on Primo, reinforced by your spur only if necessary), and (3) stop bracing with the right rein. Instead, open it a little more.

  That moves Primo's front end to the right. Now you need to move his back end to the right.
- Keep your left brace rein on Primo's neck. Return the right rein to its original position (namely, braced about 3 inches from his neck). This shuts his front doors.

- Move your left leg about 8 inches behind the girth and continue to keep your right leg off Primo's side.
- Shift your weight to the left and push with your left seatbone and your left leg. This plus another "Over" opens his right back door.
- Repeat the front end / back end sequence until Primo has moved a couple of steps to the right. Don't ask him for too much at first. Concentrate on correct cues. Stay slow.
- Close the doors on the opened side by bringing your leg and rein back to a normal position, then *use the in-neutral cues to end the movement*. It's just as important to have a clear way to end the movement as it is to start it. Otherwise, you will not have complete control. This applies to everything you ask Primo to do, whether you ask in the saddle or on the ground. Again I remind you that Primo should respond to *you*, not to the situation.

For a sidepass to the left, change right to left. Practice sidepasses in both directions. A video should show Primo crossing over first in front, then in back (as for doing a turn on the foreleg, then on the haunches). Then, on the side he's passing toward, he'll move that front and back leg over before repeating each crossover.

When Primo's crossovers become easier for him and you, it's time to ask him for additional steps. That's when you'll start working toward the goal of being able to sidepass *both ends simultaneously* whenever he feels your leg about 4 inches behind the girth. (Four inches is halfway between being *at* the girth and 8 inches *behind* the girth.) Do this by reducing how far up or back you put your leg to ask Primo to move his front and back ends. Do it maybe half an inch at a time.

Flexing to a Leading Rein

Pal responds to Teresa's leading left rein by flexing his head to the left. Teresa proves you can rein two-handed (even cue with a leading rein) on a curbed bit with fixed shanks by using careful hands. She also shows an indirect right rein. And here you see the left side of Pal's one-ear–style headstall. The loop goes over his right ear.

Meanwhile, reduce your leading rein cue. Do not change your brace rein (on the opposite side). And keep your leg off the side Primo moves toward. This keeps the doors closed on one side and opened on the other side.

Asking for a Front Crossover Step

Teresa's right leg cues Pal at the cinch. Imagine her right seatbone pushing. You can see her weight shifted slightly to her left. The reins tell Pal not to go forward or to the right. It's hard for us to read the reins from this angle, but they seem to say "Go left." Pal's ears tell us he's listening to Teresa. She's asking him to move his right foreleg to the left. This crossover step could be for a turn on the haunches or the front part of a sidepass.

Front Crossover
Pal responds to Teresa and moves his right foreleg under his body behind his left foreleg. *Note:* For a crossover in back, she would cue him behind the girth. This would start a turn on the foreleg or the back part of a sidepass.

As you work on these little changes, think and use the verbal cue "Over" each time you want Primo to move sideways.

When you and Primo have reached the point where he can sidepass four or five steps in either direction, it's time to go back to using your in-neutral stops. Every time you include a stop (or a check), you enforce your control of Primo.

Tip: If you're having trouble getting Primo's "doors" to respond to your leg and weight cues, maybe it's because you twist or squeeze and make your seatbones counteract what your legs say. Think of cues the way Primo would feel or view them. Practice giving cues while sitting on your hands. This lets you feel what Primo's back feels. Do your seatbones "agree" with what your legs are asking?

Controlling Primo with One-Handed Reining

You'll probably show Primo on the bit, which requires one-handed reining. Stay with two-handed reining until you can control him for the moves I've described. Although you may use a snaffle or bosal, you can also use a curbed bit with a loose mouthpiece (meaning the shanks are flexible, not fixed). Start your switch by holding both reins in one hand. Your leg, weight and verbal cues will stay the same.

Switch your reining cues for lateral work gradually. Follow the same plan you used for bringing your leg cues to a mid-point for a sidepass. Practice will show you how much pressure to use on Primo. You'll switch from a combination of brace and *leading* rein to a combination of brace and *neck* rein. Your goal is to switch from using a leading rein on one side to using a neck rein on the opposite side.

Use whatever bit Primo works best for, provided it's allowed in the rules. This applies to any and all riding activities. However, to quote noted trainer Sam Powell, "Regardless of what you put in a horse's mouth, it can't work any better than the person pulling the reins."

Obstacles

Now that you have the necessary controls over Primo, we'll go on to obstacles. Trail classes have a certain number of mandatory obstacles, then the judges may select from a list of optional ones to complete the course. Read the trail section in the rule book of the organization that sanctions the show you plan to enter. Know what's mandatory, what's optional and what's unacceptable (this can vary). Some clubs offer very helpful study sheets that describe the trail course.

Trail obstacles offer variety and mental challenge, which are ideal for keeping horses from getting bored or sour. A horse will tune out his rider after so much drill on Western pleasure. On the other hand, horses that get too excited after performing faster activities (such as reining, Western riding or even barrel racing) can often be calmed down by doing trail work. It slows them down and makes them think.

Before we discuss obstacles, here's some advice:

- Protect Primo's front legs before schooling over obstacles. This could prevent bruises, cuts or splinters if he bumps something. Ask an expert to help you select and then put boots or leg wraps on him properly.
- Collect obstacles (poles, barrels, cones, tires and objects that have to be built, which are described later in this chapter) and gradually add them to Primo's daily environment so he won't be afraid of them.

Move them around or just stack them, but keep as many objects as possible visible and (under safe conditions) available. Once Primo starts working with objects, do what you can to change their appearance so he'll keep paying attention to your signals.

- While schooling, stop and relax Primo after he's acted upon an obstacle nicely, then go on to another. Don't change the *way* you want him to take obstacles, but do change the *order* in which you take them. This keeps Primo from wanting to rush from one to the next. Mix trail with rail work, and include obstacles as part of Primo's warm-up in your daily schooling as well as before a show class.

- If you're using trail work as a warm-up before a pleasure class, leave your stirrups alone. Otherwise, shorten them a notch or two. They should be long enough to let you take a deep seat, comfortable for a normal (basic balanced) seat, yet short enough to give security and balance while riding in a two-point position. You'll use all three seats for trail work.

Step-overs

Step-overs are usually ground poles, 8 to 12 feet long and at least 4 inches thick. Railroad ties are thicker, much heavier and quite sturdy. They can be used as elementary step-overs, but are even more useful for holding elevated step-overs. (Trainer Penny Gibbs suggests putting notches in the ties every 15 inches, so you'll be able to skip a set of notches as needed to get the right distance between poles. Use the notches as "cups" for the poles to rest in.) Most riders use poles of solid wood that are similar to those used for jumping. Some trainers prefer starting off with unpainted wood, but Primo is a finished horse. He shouldn't be bothered by white or colorful poles any more than he'd object to painted barrels. *Remove any sharp edges from any object Primo steps over.* You will need help, particularly if a chain saw or circular saw is used. But someone first needs to remove all the "lumps and bumps" from the obstacle being built. After that, you can sand it smooth. Plastic pipe (called PVC, available in 10-foot lengths) is less expensive than lumber for making stepovers. However, plastic is lightweight and easily cracked. In the long run, you are probably better off investing in 4 × 4-inch wood beams and / or railroad ties. Or perhaps you can get lumber from freshly cut trees. (I prepared several poles from sapling oak trees that my husband had cut down while clearing land for a new pasture.)

You should be able to begin by asking Primo to walk over a single ground pole and not meet any resistance. (You could also probably start out with one-handed reining, but let's use two hands at first.) Walk him toward the center of the pole in a straight line. When you get two or three steps away, bump the reins to get his attention.

As soon as you've bumped the reins, assume a two-point position, as for jumping. (You don't need to lean forward as much at this slow speed.) Lifting your seatbones off the saddle lightens Primo's back and makes it easier for him to lift his back legs enough not to hit the pole with his feet.

Just before Primo picks up his front feet, he may want to lower his head and check the pole. Be ready for this and allow your hands to follow him down. Consider yourself lucky. Judges give Primo credit for looking first, then going ahead. (He should do this before crossing any forward obstacle, but not for backward or lateral moves.)

If Primo hesitates too long, use leg pressure to encourage him to go forward. Don't give him bad ideas (bad think-talk) by expecting him to balk. If you feel him get tense or begin to draw back, cluck and start driving him forward. If you react soon enough by urging him on, you can avoid a fight. Be sure to keep your two-point position until after both of Primo's back feet have stepped over. Your legs will feel his back legs lift and come down.

Once he's across, resume a normal seat. For the first few times across, drop the reins to neutral and say "Whoa." Then praise him. It was just a little step-over, but his doing it increased your bond, making you more of a team.

As long as Primo does what you ask without rushing or avoiding the step-overs, you must be doing it right. Try stepping over at a jog, then a lope. Add a pole and go through all the gaits again. Then add another pole, go through all the gaits and so forth until you've worked up to four or more poles. Change the distance between your poles. Rules vary. Besides, this is a good way to keep Primo's attention. As a general guide, set the poles 15 to 24 inches apart for walk-overs, 24 to 42 inches apart for jog-overs and 6 to 7 feet apart for lope-overs.

Carefully study all the trail rules for the shows you plan to enter. This lets you know what to expect. For example, AQHA says that for poles to be trotted or loped over, they must be flat on the ground, not elevated.

Work with two poles for quite a while before adding the third and fourth. That second pole is harder for you and Primo to learn how to rate than all the rest. ("Rate" can have different meanings. Here, and also for jumping, it means to figure how fast and far apart to make each stride from point A to point B. You may have to adjust in order to come exactly upon point B—not too short or too far. For example, say you know the distance from A to B. Say Primo's stride is stabilized.

You rate by counting his strides between A and B. "Rate" is used in Chapter 7 to mean "check," as in slowing Primo to be ready to do something different. It's used yet another way in roping events, as you'll see in Chapter 8.)

Sometimes the poles are laid out in a spiral pattern (flat or elevated) instead of being parallel. This can be easy and fun, or scary, depending on how you think. Here's the easy way to school for elevated spiral (fanlike) poles:

- Start with one pole elevated at one end. You can make a fancy holder out of a 50-gallon drum with holes big enough to hold the poles. Or, you can simply prop one end of the pole on a tire, and maybe vary the size of tire. Circle the drum or tire several times. Get into a pattern so you'll always cross over the same spot. Mark your spot lightly with chalk.
- Add more poles, then use just enough leg and open rein to keep Primo moving. Let him work his way through. Let him do it several times. Sooner or later, he'll cross each pole at the same spot that's right for his stride at that gait. He won't hit a pole. Chalk those spots (or ask someone who sees the spot to do it).
- Go off and do something else. When you come back to the obstacle, the marks will guide you through learning to follow a steadily curved, not round, path. You'll enter and leave at a given point. If your path goes off course, the poles' spacing and height will change.
- When Primo can go through without hitting a pole, turn the poles over to hide the chalk marks and go again. This teaches you to rely on your judgment for lining him up.

If Primo keeps hitting poles, examine your riding. Ask a good rider to watch (or, better, to videotape) you. Maybe you need to practice lungeing in a two-point position. Your legs and lower back must hold you strong and secure at two-point so that you won't lean on your hands (pull on the reins for balance). Maybe you lean your head over to look down at the pole instead of staying level and looking ahead to where you want Primo to go. Either fault can break Primo's rhythm and cause him to hit the poles.

Sometimes the problem is not caused by anything you're doing wrong. If Primo tends to go crooked, use more leg or rein pressure on whichever side moves out.

Maybe Primo simply doesn't lift his feet high enough. You can correct this laziness by using your legs (plus seatbones until just before going two-point) to drive him more. Practice will tell whether you must also adjust the reins to rate him at the proper speed. If he hits the poles because of rushing, however, you need to go back to basics. You know what that means. Put him in neutral after stepping over one pole, then *gradually* add more poles and speed.

Some shows use tires as step-overs. Most associations classify tires as unacceptable because a horse might get his foot trapped and panic. I personally don't see any great danger to using tires as step-overs, as long as the horse is calm and well trained and especially if he's ridden by someone whose control he trusts and obeys. Use the same cues as you'd use for poles. After Primo has had his look, ask him to step in and then out as he crosses over the tire (or tires).

If low jumps are included, refer to the section on jumping in Chapter 3 and add that information to what you've learned here about stepping over ground poles. You should be able to handle taking low jumps in a stock-seat saddle.

Water Obstacles

A *water obstacle* can be a puddle, a pond or a shallow creek, a box lined with a plastic sheet and filled with water or even a weighted-down plastic sheet *without* water. The water's never any deeper than Primo's knees and more often it's just 2 to 3 inches deep.

Horse are rarely born afraid of water. But if Primo is afraid of getting his feet wet, you can get him over this fear all by yourself. (Nevertheless, better have a buddy nearby, just in case.)

Don't wait to encounter water while you're out riding to learn how Primo reacts. Find a puddle or a pool of water no deeper than 4 inches and at least 4 feet in diameter. If it's too small, Primo can step over it. You want him to step *in* it. Bring a carrot or other treat you know Primo likes. Bring rubber boots, too. Set the treat beyond the puddle and go get Primo. After some grooming and hugging to put him in a good mood, calmly lead him to the puddle.

Here's where real horse psychology comes in. In order to assure Primo that he really does want to walk through the puddle, *you* have to walk through it first. Don't tense up (in case you forgot the rubber boots). Primo will notice. For the same reason, don't stomp in the water and make a big splash. You need a lead rope that's long enough to let you go first. Stand next to Primo, stroke his neck and talk to him while you both look down at the water. As soon as he seems relaxed, you step in. Stand in the water and cluck for Primo to move. Don't stand there and face him, though. Turn and calmly walk to the other side, think-talking what you want Primo to do. He should let you lead him through the water. If he does, reward him. If he resists being led through, don't lose your temper. But don't reward him.

Before he saw you step in the water first, Primo might not have wanted to step in because he can't see to judge bottom. He can't tell whether the water is 2 inches or 2 feet deep. You'd have been unfair, therefore, to force him in if that's why he didn't want to go. By going in first, you gave him reason to trust and follow you when asked.

This simple method I've described will almost always work. It will work on a horse who wasn't afraid of water to begin with. And it will work on a horse who was a confirmed water-hater until he saw you walk through water unhurt.

Primo may react to water another way. He may try to rush through or even jump over the puddle. Usually you can see this coming. He may tremble or snort, then get ready to spring. If Primo does this, calmly but quickly return to his side and take him for a little stroll on dry land. When you feel him relax, return to the water and try again. Keep a shorter hold on the line for more control.

Another way to get him across is to have someone lead another horse through first, then you and Primo follow. A buddy nearby is also good for when you ride him across. But try not to involve anyone else unless you have to. You want Primo to respond to *you and your controls.*

Remember, it's best that you lead Primo calmly through a water obstacle before riding him through. When he does carry you through, reward him generously. Then take him through once more before going on to something else. When you're out in the open, take advantage of every puddle and other water that's safe to cross, or enter, without soaking your boots or saddle.

If Primo starts trying to rush across, put him in neutral as soon as he gets all four feet in the water. Or, if it's a small puddle, when his front feet are in. Make him stand there a minute while you praise him. Do this from time to time (but not *every* time).

Primo might not want to enter water because the footing appears unsafe. If you sense that he wants to go in, but he really seems worried about the footing, lead him around to a different spot that somehow feels right. This is a perfect example of Primo think-talking to you, with a good response.

Fear of unsafe footing can cause problems if the "water hazard" in a trail class is a plastic sheet with the edges held down by dirt. Plastic sheets smell strange, make strange noises and may even slide when stepped on. You can understand why Primo might not want to step on it.

But you can convince him to do it. Prepare a fake puddle, then follow the same plan as for a real puddle. If you have a dog that gets along well with Primo, let the dog demonstrate by walking on the plastic sheet. (Before you let Primo see this, run a test. You may find that your dog hesitates and sniffs it a lot before walking on it, too.)

Crossing Bridges

Until you've crossed a bridge with Primo, you don't know how he'll respond. Therefore, it's best not to start out across a real bridge spanning a full river. A more cautious approach would begin with a 4 × 8-foot plywood sheet (at least ½ inch thick, so Primo won't step right through it) placed flat on the ground. Lay the plywood where Primo can see it every day and have a good chance to study it on his own. Follow the water-crossing plan to lead Primo across the plywood, then ride him over it. Once you have him walking over the board in a relaxed manner, and getting used to how it sounds, graduate to a wooden bridge. Occasionally put him in neutral midway over.

When Primo crosses a bridge, wades through water or walks on pavement or plastic, the footing feels and sounds different to him than being on solid ground. But a well-broke horse should be able to handle different surfaces.

You'll probably hear all kinds of scare stories about bridges from other riders. No doubt they made mistakes and then blamed their horses. Your only problem might be if Primo had had a bad bridge experience before you got him.

The quickest way to get over a bad bridge experience is also the best way to avoid having one. Go back to basics. In this case, go back to walking over the plywood flat on the ground. Success is then a matter of your control over Primo and his trusting you.

Sidepassing an Obstacle

Before you try this sidepassing an obstacle, first Primo must be able to sidepass in both directions, mainly in response to your leg and seatbone cues, although you'll also cue with the reins. In addition to asking him to move sideways, you'll ask him to accept the presence of an object between his front and back legs.

We'll start with a single ground pole.

Ride Primo alongside one end of the pole and stop him when the pole is midway between his front and back legs. The easiest way for you to line him up from the saddle is to look down your leg at the pole. Raise your leg straight out if you can't quite see your foot. The pole should be at your heel or barely behind it. That's where it needs to stay for Primo to sidepass it without hitting it. If it's not right there, move him ahead or back a step before giving him the side-pass signals.

When Primo has made enough sideways cross-over steps to be directly over the pole, put him in neutral and ask him to stand for several seconds. This serves two purposes. It reminds Primo that you're in control (so he won't rush), and it gives you a chance to check his position over the pole. (You won't disturb his carefully balanced moves by looking.)

Put Primo in gear, make any necessary adjustments, and continue sidepassing. Stop and check again when you're about halfway down the pole, then continue to the other end. Stop and look down your opposite leg to check your position, then use the same method for returning to where you started.

There's really nothing scary about sidepassing over an object. Your ways of controlling Primo's sidepass are the same whether the path is clear of objects or if there's a grounded or elevated pole between his front and back legs. For sidepassing an L turn, follow the same technique, but add a slow, careful turn on the foreleg to move his hindquarters around the corner, or vice versa.

The three keys to avoiding trouble with sidepassing are (1) keep Primo slow, (2) check your position often and (3) protect his legs. Primo's more likely to hit the pole if he gets in a hurry, but he can hit it for other reasons, too.

Back-Throughs

Back-throughs are patterns that Primo must follow in reverse gear, getting from point A to point B (and sometimes C, D and beyond). A simple back-through obstacle is two parallel ground poles. Even though they lie on the ground, think of the poles as forming a sort of tunnel that Primo must back out of. Practice first by having the poles about 4 feet apart, then gradually narrow the "tunnel." Minimum width is 28 inches.

Those same three keys to avoiding trouble with sidepassing also apply to taking him successfully through a back-through. In addition, here are two schooling tricks for helping you line up the obstacle he will back through.

1. Ride Primo forward through the poles, stop when his hind feet are still inside, then cue him to back up. This gives Primo a chance to see the ground poles before he's asked to back through them and minimizes your chances of starting him off crooked.

2. Check your position by sighting down one side only. Don't twist one way, then the other, to see where Primo's feet are in relation to where the poles are because this can shift his hindquarters off-center. Keep your body straight and evenly weighted in the saddle, and keep your head as level as possible while you glance down. You'll start off by having Primo in the middle. Then, as long as you keep the spacing consistent on *one* side while backing, the space on the *other* side will automatically be the same.

Square turns on back-throughs are more advanced but no more difficult than straight backing. Here's how to do it:

- Line up and back Primo straight, sighting for space consistency on the side where the corner will be.
- Put him in neutral when the inside corner appears to be just below his flank (or your marker for that spot).
- Use your outside leg to turn his hindquarters over and into the next "tunnel." (This is an inside turn on the foreleg.)

- Once his hips are inside the next segment of the obstacle, move your inside leg up and ask him to move his shoulders over to clear the corner. (This is an outside turn on the hindquarters).

Each of these moves will only be a step or two, with a neutral wait in between. This allows you to turn your head slightly and gauge where everything is. Be sure you're evenly balanced again before putting Primo in gear.

Negotiating curving turns through back-throughs requires more lateral flexibility of Primo. (Forward or backward, picture him "bending around your leg.") First practice backing a curved path without obstacles. Control Primo while backing in a circle and in serpentines before trying an obstacle. Here's how to bend him to the right, one-handed:

- First, place your right leg at the girth.
- Then use a soft high left neck rein for asking Primo to flex his poll so you can see the corner of his right eye. Keep that rein steady and softly say "Whoa."
- Move your left leg about 6 inches behind the girth so you can move his haunches to the right, but don't apply pressure yet.
- Now ask Primo to "Back" and use your left leg to push his haunches around. Pause in neutral between moves. Change left for right to back around the other direction.

After you become more experienced at these moves, work on getting Primo in position to back through the obstacle without walking forward through it first. There are different ways of doing this. Here's one way:

- Determine how much room it takes for Primo to do a 90-degree (quarter-circle) turn on the foreleg.

- Allow that much space, plus about a foot, when you ride up to the mouth of the obstacle. The obstacle will be at your side, as if you were going to sidepass it.
- Use one of the two obstacles (probably the front one) that you'll back through as a marker for where to line up your saddle horn or maybe your boot.
- When Primo's lined up, do a turn on the foreleg to get him in position to start his back-through.

Only practice will give the information you'll need to judge space. And practice will also show you how to pick markers for positioning Primo to back or sidepass.

Let's set him up to turn during a back-through as an example. You might line up the corner of the turn with your front saddle concho. Maybe you'll sight it by the zigzag on the front or back edge of your blanket. You must find all your own markers. Their locations will vary according to Primo's size and your size.

Study the rules for descriptions of what Primo might be asked to negotiate. You'll be able to back him through any obstacle by using some combination of the methods I've just described. Take your time, plan ahead and use think-talk.

The Turnaround Box

The *turnaround box* tests Primo's ability to revolve a full circle inside tight space. To do this, he must rotate around a midway point of his body. The box can be as small as 5 feet square, but usually it's 6 feet square. Start off schooling with one that's 8 to 12 feet square and gradually reduce the size.

Before you step into the box, check Primo's responses to turning cues by doing a couple of turns on the haunches and forehand. If he's listening, here's how you'll proceed:

- Enter the box by asking Primo to step over the pole while you're in two-point position. Drop your reins to neutral as soon as you feel his back feet land inside.
- For rotating to the right, put Primo in gear and move his front end one step to the right, then put him in neutral.
- Put him in gear and move his back end one step to the left, then put him in neutral again.
- Gradually move his front end another step to the right, then his hindquarters another step to the left, and so on, until Primo has rotated the full 360 degrees.
- Raise your two-point position to step out of the circle, and praise Primo before going on to something else.

Gates

There are several correct ways to go through a gate on Primo. However, you are penalized by changing hands or by losing contact with the gate. When the gate opens *away* from you, you can use a right-hand *push*. Here's how to go through a gate when the opening is on the left:

- Approach the gate from the right so Primo is parallel to it. Move him forward until his head is just past the latch, then stop him. Reach over and unlatch the gate with your off hand. Keep your hand on the gate.
- As you back Primo a step or two, lean on your hand to push the gate partly open.
- When Primo's head clears the gatepost, turn his head into the opening and walk him through. Your hand will automatically open the gate wide enough to pass through.

- When your right leg is on the other side of the gate, use that leg to push Primo's haunches around to the left.
- Use your left leg to move his front end over to the right to get him straight.
- Ask Primo for a step or two forward to get closer. Then shut and latch the gate. Praise Primo and ride on.

Here's how to *pull* that gate open from the other side:

- Line up parallel with the gate, with the latch at your left leg.
- Unlatch the gate with your left hand and pull it toward you.
- At the same time, use your left leg to turn his haunches to the right (turn on the foreleg) a quarter circle. This will arc him around the gate so that he faces the opening.
- Walk him forward until his back leg clears the gate.
- Move his rear to the right again until he's parallel with the gate. Back him a step or two so you can latch it.

Trade left for right if the gate fastens on the right.

You'll find other ways to open and pass through gates. For example, Primo might prefer to back through, then turn.

Other Obstacles

You can use what you've learned to help Primo negotiate other trail obstacles. Using the same logic, you can also figure out how to get him positioned so you can open a mail box, carry an object from A to B, or put on and take off a slicker. This just leaves learning how to ground-tie Primo and how to put hobbles on him. I suggest getting individual help from an expert on how to tie Primo's front legs loosely together with a hobble line. Get this person to show you how it's done, then do it yourself.

Ground-tied means Primo is trained not to move after his reins have been dropped or laid on the ground. If you've done your homework with verbal commands, it's easier to ground-tie Primo than to hobble him. Dismount and loop the ends of his split reins on the ground beneath his neck. Say "Whoa" and then walk a complete circle around him. Or tell him "Whoa" once when you get off to turn up the cuffs of your chaps, then think-talk it again as you leave. Make no sudden moves, but don't walk overly slow, like you're dreading Primo might move. (That's negative think-talk.) Walk around his hindquarters first. Primo would more likely want to move if you approached his head first.

Primo's reins are "tied to the ground" by your command. He stays until you return and "untie" him. When you school at home, desensitize Primo by making him stand while other riders move around in the arena. Be reasonable about how long you leave him "tied." Be generous with praise when he obeys you. But don't always reward him with a treat. His expecting a treat could cause problems at a show.

How Problems Can Develop

Bo tries to get Delight to turn on her haunches. Usually this is no
problem. This time, however, they get into a fight. Here's why: first,
it's raining hard when everybody arrives at the CCC Equine Center.
Bo's mother parks the trailer under a shed. Faced with getting wet
before the picture-taking session or not warming up, Bo chooses to
stay under the shed instead of riding on the grass for a warm-up.
Delight steps out of the trailer into a strange place. She probably
senses everybody's concern about the bad weather. Then she's
immediately asked to turn on her haunches. No way! Bo shouldn't
blame Delight for misbehaving. Besides, the footing is terrible. The
ground is hard and unlevel, with big scary rocks that move under her
feet.

Communication

Here's a picture of think-talk and body-talk by both horse and rider!
Bo and Delight "talk things over" and work out their communication
problems. Moments later, the rain stops. The sun comes out. We can
take pictures. (Notice Bo's bridle headstall. Compare its brow band
and throatlatch with Teresa's one-ear style. Both show bridles have
silver trim and handsome matching breast collars, not shown here.)

Backing Through a Gate

Most Quarter Horse riders go forward through a gate, which I've
described in the text. But Bo prefers backing through. First, he puts
the reins down in neutral position. Then he leans down and opens
the gate.

Backing Through a Gate

Bo picks the reins up in gear. Then his right leg cues Delight to move her rear to the left. (The mare on the other side of the fence is a stranger to Delight. So far, Delight concentrates on Bo.)

Backing Through a Gate

Once he's backed through, Bo moves Delight's rear to the left again.

Backing Through a Gate
Just as Bo pushes the gate shut, the mare nickers a friendly greeting and steals Delight's attention from Bo.

Backing Through a Gate
Delight stands quietly while Bo fastens the gate. Meanwhile, she watches the approching foal. (However, Bo wisely moves before the foal reaches the fence. Sure enough, the mama—who seems here to be paying no attention to Delight—suddenly rushes to the fence and protectively cries, "Get away from my baby!")

Checking an Obstacle

Here's Delight's Tennessee Walking Horse version of checking a stepover. She keeps her head up, flexing her poll more instead of lowering her head to investigate something on the ground. Notice the slack reins and Bo's two-point position.

Checking an Obstacle

Here's Pal's Quarter Horse version of checking a stepover. The slack rein and Teresa's position show that she's urging Pal to step over the pole.

Crossing a Bridge

We made this bridge by folding up a "coop jump." Notice the bridge tilt under Pal's weight as he obediently steps on something he's never set foot on before. His expression, especially his eyes, say he's a little worried about this.

Crossing a Bridge

Teresa puts her reins "in neutral" to stop Pal midway across. Then she loses his attention briefly to something he sees across the pasture. She's smiling here, amused at her equine friend—who is clearly no longer worried.

Crossing a Bridge
The bridge tilts again as Pal steps off the end.

CHAPTER 5

———◆●◆———

Equitation Classes

In a Western horsemanship, stock-seat equitation or hunt-seat equitation class you are judged, not Primo. How you sit and use your natural aids, especially your hands, to control Primo is very important. These equitation classes are more than just rail classes. As you'll see when I describe the tests, they're definitely influenced by reining. You can't simply sit on Primo in an ideal pose. You really must be able to ride and to show control of him while doing specific required movements.

You are also judged for your ability to deal with Primo's unexpected movements. Say, for example, another rider loses control of her horse during a test. Primo was quietly lined up at the rail waiting his turn, but he shies when the horse nearly runs over him. If you quickly regain control of Primo, the judge will credit you for what you did instead of faulting Primo for what he did. As for the other rider, it depends on the degree of danger and size of class. She may lose points or be "given the gate" (excused from the class).

What Is the Perfect Horse for Equitation?

Primo needs to be smooth-moving and have gaits that make it easy for you to hold your position. He needs to round his back and work more off his hindquarters than his front end. His poll should be slightly above the height of his withers, his nose just ahead of vertical.

Primo's size and temperament should suit a person of your size and general level of experience. A little girl perched on a big-barreled horse, her legs stuck straight out, may make a cute picture, but she'd ride better if the horse were smaller and her legs could drop down. She can't drive him into the bit if her legs are so short that they're unable to bend for contacting his sides.

The Basic Position for Equitation

Keep your seat in the saddle at all times, except when you're asked to post a trot. Ideally, your head and shoulders stay level and almost motionless. Your legs stay relatively motionless also—no foot swinging. Only your lower back moves with Primo. This body movement is not counted against you because you are moving *with* your horse as you match CB/weight with him. Doing it, your back appears nearly flat. You look relaxed and comfortable.

The best exercise for developing a good equitation seat is to ride without stirrups and be lunged without reins. You've already ridden without stirrups to improve your balance. It's also excellent for strengthening your back and legs. In order to hold yourself in a straight line from ear to heel when you ride any faster than a walk or jog, you need real body strength. You need it for driving Primo and to stay with him in fast moves (such as stops and spins).

When you ride without stirrups, your legs come down so your calves touch the girth area. This generally happens automatically when you adjust yourself to keep balanced without stirrups. That's also the proper place for your calves *with* stirrups. It puts your calves where you can promptly cue Primo by rolling them in. Don't stick your calves out off Primo's sides for equitation. Don't try to pull your calves back and pressure his sides by bending your knees. And don't tighten your seat muscles. This flexes the wrong places. Start flexing at your hips and on down your thighs. (Adjust your "pliers.")

A level on-the-crotch seat is the position you want for equitation. However, it doesn't work unless your back and legs are strong enough to hold you in place when Primo moves faster than is required for pleasure or trail class. Otherwise, if you lack enough strength and / or riding experience, your upper body will tip forward.

The answer to this problem is to modify your position. Roll back on your seatbones (rather than sit in the middle of your crotch) and put your legs slightly forward (rather than straight down). This deeper seat makes it easier for you to keep your upper body still and straight. It prepares you better to use what you have to drive Primo and to stay with him during faster moves. Eventually, as you grow and gain strength as a rider, you won't need this modification.

You want your stirrups as long as possible but not so long that they don't give you some support. Don't put a lot of weight in your stirrups. Too much weight in the stirrups tends to push your crotch out of the saddle and the stirrups out to the sides. When you push, do it without raising your heels higher than your toes. If your heels come up, it's probably because you need to relax your legs and deepen your seat. But you may just need to shorten your stirrups.

Picture an imaginary line to the ground passing through your ear, shoulder, hip and heel. Then imagine Primo being erased from under your seat. A perfect equitation position would leave you standing normally on the ground, except for a slight bend to the knees and lowered heels. (Do you line up when your feet hang free, but your heels move forward with your feet in the stirrup? Your stirrups probably need to be repositioned. This can be done at a saddle shop.)

Lift your neck; don't keep it buried in your collar. Let it rise out of shoulders that are held level, backward and down, not rounded forward. Train your shoulders, neck and jaw to relax. Practice rotating your neck and shoulders in big circles, as you do for the ankle exercise. As for your jaw, the best exercise is to smile. Don't frown from concentrating too hard, either. If you relax and smile, you'll tend to do everything else right and have that WTB look. If you don't, you'll tend to be tense everywhere else, including your hands. Primo, of course, will feel this and also become tense.

You'll rein with just one hand, but hold both hands and arms in a relaxed easy manner. Both upper arms should be in line with your body, not ahead of or behind it. Your rein arm should bend at the elbow, forming a straight line from the elbow through the rein to Primo's mouth. This can't be done with reins held as slack as is sometimes seen in Western pleasure. Therefore, keep light contact (2 to 3 inches of slack) for controlling Primo. Use your fingers and wrist for making most rein adjustments. Some arm movement is permissible, but jerking and excess pumping loses points.

Hold the reins 1½ to 2 inches over and in front of the pommel. That's just enough to clear the horn without touch-

Riding a Tennessee Walker Western Style

Overall, Bo's head and body position are quite nice. I like his pleasant, confident expression. His plain denim jeans are okay, but chaps or longer pants would be better for show. Bo's back is excellent—straight and flat without being stiff. His ear, shoulder, hip and ankle line up perfectly with the telephone pole. However, even though Bo is using his right calf to keep Delight in a big circle to the left, he should drop his right heel slightly. His left heel is more flexible than his right one. In fact, Bo's entire left leg is more relaxed than his right leg. Drawing circles with both feet could help "equalize" his legs and make his right ankle more flexible. Delight, meanwhile, performs her natural running walk. Slower and more relaxed than the "big lick" show gait this breed is noted for, it is flashy and much faster than the typical Western walk.

ing it. Keep your reining wrist straight and relaxed whenever possible, with your thumb on top and fingers closed around the reins. Do this whether the reins enter between your thumb and index finger then exit under your little finger

About Fitting the Rider to the Horse

Here is how a little girl perched on a big horse can look cute and also have everything fit . . . except for Sarah's hat, which is too big. (Be sure your hat fits properly. You should feel the skin under your hair move slightly when you wiggle your safety helmet with the chin strap fastened.) When Sarah stands next to Arizona, the lowest part of his back is taller than she is. When mounted, her feet barely reach a line straight back from his point of shoulder. However, because Arizona's barrel is fairly narrow, Sarah's legs don't stick out at the sides like she's doing splits. Because of this, she is able to use her legs in a normal manner for good control.

Riding the Jog and Turning

Arizona has been jogging in a circle to the right. Here Sarah asks him to turn left. His next stride will be to the left. You can see how Sarah really puts her whole self into telling Arizona exactly what she wants him to do. You can also see (judging by the telephone pole) how well she sits.

(split-rein style) or vice versa (romal style). For split reins, you may put one finger between the reins if the reins fall on the near side. They *must* fall on the near side for APHA. (In this case, "near" means the same side as your rein hand, left or right.) No finger is allowed between the reins when using a romal rein or, for AHSA, if the split ends fall on the off side and are held like a romal.

If using a romal, your off hand should be around the romal with at least 16 inches of rein between your hands. (This doesn't mean your hands must be 16 inches apart.) The position of your off hand is optional, as long as it doesn't touch Primo or the saddle. For holding the rein ends or a romal, balance your fist (or just your wrist) lightly on your

Riding the Gallop

Sarah is in absolute harmony with Arizona as she urges him into a gallop. She sits in a secure three-point position for reining that's also correct for equitation, especially for a small person riding a big horse. She could use a two-point position during Arizona's gallop if she wanted. It would put her weight/CB more forward, which is needed for speed events such as barrel racing and roping.

thigh. When using split reins, you may also place your off fist on your thigh. But many judges prefer that you bend your off elbow and hold your off hand to match your reining hand. This position helps you keep your shoulders level. A good rule is to keep your empty fist relaxed just enough to hide an imaginary small ball. Don't squeeze your fist shut or lock your arm down. This looks tense. If you open your fist or let your arm hang straight down, this looks too casual. Finally, don't clutch your fist to your stomach like you have a pain.

Transitions

One thing the judge will really look for is how you signal Primo's transitions. The ability to produce smooth transitions is a mark of good horsemanship. Changing from one gait to another is a challenge to Primo's balance as well as to your own balance and skill.

Primo's head tells a lot about what's happening with him, particularly with his hindquarters. As you learned in Chapter 1, when Primo moves forward, he keeps losing his balance and regaining it by counterbalancing. The more collected he is, the less his head has to move with each stride to regain his balance. Therefore, you can see why it's foolish to try to improve Primo's way of going by correcting his head-set. Correct his *body* and his head will take care of itself.

The best way to correct Primo's body is by keeping *your* body balanced and by driving him with your legs and seat-bones. This makes him round his back and reach under his body with his back feet. (In Chapter 2 we called this being vertically engaged.) You'll also use your weight. Even slight body shifts are important for asking transitions. Keep Primo straight. Never ask him for a transition while he's crooked.

Andy Moorman is a well-known trainer. She, too, likes to use mental pictures for teaching various techniques to young riders. For example, she uses the "flamingo" exercise. As her students stand on the ground, she asks them to stand first on one leg and then the other, like a flamingo. After they've done this, she asks them to do it again, but without shifting their weight. Now try it yourself. I bet you lost your balance and nearly fell over! As you just found out, you have to make some important self-adjustments, even if they're tiny. Your own small but vital adjustments must happen before Primo can have balanced, smooth transitions.

Before you ask for any transition, you need to warn Primo, to get his attention. For an upward transition, start by barely closing your fingers (lightly bump the reins). Follow this by fluttering your calves to energize his body. This tells him the front door is about to open. Or, if it's already open, it will open wider. For a downward transition, reverse the process. Bump with your legs, then catch Primo's energy with your hands by lightly bumping the reins. This tells him the front door is about to close.

From Walk to Jog or Trot

Before you move from a walk to a jog or trot, deepen your seat and bring your weight back just a little. This asks Primo to bring his hind legs further under his body. Next, get his attention. You'll feel him grow a little taller as he rounds his back. As soon as you feel this, add a little more leg (use your calf) and let his energy come through as a jog. The trick is to bump the reins just enough to make him listen, then release them so that he'll soften at the poll and promptly pick up the jog. It's a matter of timing that only practice can show you.

If you want Primo to trot, use a little more leg. Then, as he goes faster, pick up your diagonal and begin posting. (For the proper diagonal, rise with the outside front leg or sit when the inside front leg is up. Doing either will have the same result. Do whichever is easier for you.) Only by practice and listening to Primo can you learn how much leg and rein is needed to keep good impulse.

From Walk to Lope

In order to move from a walk to a lope, you first must know the gait footfall patterns and you *should* be able to feel where

Primo's feet are. To strike off on a lead, he has to push off with the opposite back foot. For a right lead, he pushes off with the left back foot. Therefore, don't ask him when he already has his weight on his left back foot. Ask when he has his weight on one of his front feet, preferably his right front foot.

I've stressed the importance of keeping your shoulders level, but it is possible to shift your shoulders slightly to one side without dropping either shoulder. By shifting your shoulders just 3 inches to whichever side is *opposite* the lead you want to ask for, you can shift enough weight onto that seatbone for Primo to feel it. This also puts you in position for flexing your calf on that side, behind the girth, to ask for a lope departure. (It uses the "flamingo" theory.) To ask for a right lead, just before you move your left leg, barely bump the right rein to alert Primo. You can bump each rein individually while riding one-handed by rolling your wrist. Don't bump too hard or Primo will think you want him to turn. You want him to stay straight. Pick the moment to flex your left calf. (Leads are covered in Chapter 6.) As you flex your calf, stretch your body upward, not forward. Do not lean forward as you ask for a lope or canter. If it's necessary for you to stand or lean forward, such as for keeping up with more speed, do this only after the canter has begun.

You'll have to experiment to find how much rein or movement is needed to keep Primo straight. If he turns, it is usually because you leaned up or over instead of staying squarely in the saddle. You want the energy generated with your legs to pass out his front door, not a side door.

As Primo pushes off into the lope, you'll feel him lift for the "across" part before he goes down for the "pull" part. As he goes down, he'll stretch his neck for balance. This is where you *must* let your elbows relax so that your hands can follow his motion. Don't make the mistake of using the reins to balance yourself. Don't stiffen your arms. Either mistake will jab Primo with the bit. As you follow with your arms, keep your shoulders down and *keep your seat in the saddle.*

Another good thing about shifting your shoulders is that it tends to keep Primo from "falling over on his inside shoulder" (leaning heavily on it). He'll do this when he's running freely in the pasture. It's okay for Primo to drop his shoulder for some speed events, but not for equitation. Try to keep Primo's hindquarters under him. They'll carry weight he would otherwise pass to his leading shoulder.

From Jog or Trot to Lope

Actually, it is easier to go from a jog to a trot or lope than it is to get Primo to lope from a walk. In fact, a green horse will usually trot a few steps during the transition from walk to lope. If you want to lope from a trot and you're posting, stop posting and sit. (You will already be sitting a jog.) Otherwise, follow the same steps you would to lope from a walk.

Downward Transitions: The Overall Approach

Not only do you lift Primo into upward transitions, you also lift him into downward transitions. Lift (bump), sit and drive. Don't think of lifting as pulling back the reins. Think of creating a barrier with your hands and then driving Primo into it. (Incidentally, this can also apply to stops.)

From Lope to Posting Trot

To go from a lope to a posting trot, keep your weight in the saddle and lift with your hands to ask Primo to listen. As you bump the reins, release your leg pressure that had kept him loping and roll up onto your crotch. When Primo feels your seatbone pressure lighten, he'll naturally *want* to trot. The moment you feel him break to the trot, start to post. If you started to post as soon as you felt his trot begin, you should automatically be on the proper diagonal. As long as you post, the rhythmic press of your legs will continue to drive him.

From Posting Trot to Jog

Lightly bump Primo to alert him to a change. Here you are moving from a posting trot to a jog. When you touch in the "down" part of posting, make contact with your crotch and then roll back to your seatbones. (Ease smoothly onto his back, matching the rhythm of his stride.) As you roll back, close your leg to keep driving Primo forward. Meanwhile, keep the same amount of bit contact. If you've kept enough steady contact with your leg and rein, and if you roll back to your seatbones, you won't get bounced. But you *will* get bounced if you stiffen your back and raise your shoulders. You'll get bounced even more if you stay perched up on your crotch. Deepen your seat. Your seatbones tell Primo to round his back. This makes his rough trot become a smooth jog. Remember, your legs (and seatbones) drive Primo's energy into your hands. If your hands don't control his front door, the energy rushes right on out.

From Lope to Walk

The only real difference between the lope-to-walk and the lope-to jog is the timing of your give-and-take with the reins. You close ("take") the reins a little longer (but not stronger) each time, as Primo comes up with each stride. Then "give" by following Primo's neck as it stretches down. This allows him to recover his balance as he slows. You'll also apply give-and-take bracing pressure with your legs. Keep quietly reapplying these aids with each stride until he comes back to an energetic walk. Then have your legs ready to keep up the walk rhythm.

If you say "Whoa," Primo should stop. Nice and easy.

Practice the full range of gait transitions during schooling sessions. Eventually your timing and feel will improve and more things will become automatic. Then (provided Primo cooperates) you can begin to loosen your reins and give Primo more freedom.

Self-Improvement

If you're learning to tell how Primo is going by feel, it's a good idea to watch a video of yourself. But because it's hard to recognize our own mistakes and see how to improve, you may want to have an expert watch with you. Whether you're a boy or a girl, a great way to see how you line up on Primo is to wear a leotard (and boots; do not ride barefooted or bareback) during one of these sessions. It will give you an accurate view of your legs and enable you to clearly see what each part of your body is doing. (This may be when you learn that you're a bit lopsided.)

Class Routine

In equitation class tests are given to each rider individually before the judge calls the top riders back for rail work. The tests are intended to challenge the rider's ability, not to exceed it. The basic pattern is posted (usually near the in-gate) at least an hour before class begins. Study it. Then mentally picture you and Primo riding through every move (perfectly, of course). When the class is called, all competitors enter the ring to hear the judge explain the pattern. Listen carefully. If you still have a question, ask it when the judge says, "Any questions?" But don't use this opportunity as a way to get his attention.

Your rule book describes all the possible tests in general. Details will vary. You should also vary how you school Primo. Horses learn patterns amazingly fast. If you always use the same reining pattern, Primo might develop the bad habit of anticipating moves. When he anticipates your moves, he does something (for example, turn or especially stop) at the point where you've done it several times before. The problem is, you haven't yet cued him to do it this time, and you may not even want him to do it this time.

Tests in General

Here's a general description of tests. Routines and procedures definitely vary among AHSA, AQHA and APHA Be sure to read the applicable rule book before showing.

1. Walk, jog, trot, lope or gallop in a straight line or on a curve or circle, or any combination of these gaits and patterns, such as a figure eight or serpentine. Sit the jog and post the trot using proper diagonals.
2. Stop. This can vary from a normal to a sliding stop.
3. Back.
4. Turn on the haunches, including spins and rollbacks, or turn on the forehand.

5. Sidepass.
6. Simple change of lead through the trot, walk or halt, in a straight line, figure eight or any other pattern.
7. Flying change of lead in a straight line, figure eight or serpentine.
8. Countercanter.
9. Dismount and mount.
10. Ride without stirrups.

Note: These test items are covered in Chapter 6:

- the sliding stop
- the spin
- the rollback
- flying lead changes
- countercanter

Cones and other markers help guide all the riders through the same pattern, but they can also increase the degree of difficulty. You have to use them. That's why they must be shown in the posted pattern. Where they are placed is carefully planned. Helpers are always ready to put a marker back if it has been knocked out of its proper place.

Each rider is given a certain period of time to complete his or her test. At the end of that time, a signal is given and the exhibitor must leave the arena even if he or she has not completed the test. Not finishing the test is not a disqualification, but it does lower a rider's score. The judge uses these scores for picking the top riders to be called back for rail work. The other riders are excused from the ring.

If you are excused, forget about it for now and get ready for your next class. Later, watch the video of your test if one was made, otherwise talk to someone who watched you ride. Then you'll know how to do better next time.

A Sample Test

Tests range from simple to complex. Here's a sample:

- Along the center line, jog to the cone. Pick up the right lead and lope five steps. From the halt, pick up the left lead and lope five steps. Halt and do one spin (full turn on the haunches) to the right or left, slow or fast. Walk from the spin to the center of the ring, facing the flag, then halt. Trot a figure eight. Halt and back four steps. Halt to indicate you've finished, then go to wherever you've been instructed to wait.
- After you do your individual work, the ring steward will ask you to wait on the rail or at the opposite end of the ring. When everybody has completed his or her test, you walk, jog and lope both directions on the rail.
- Finally, all riders line up. You'll see the judge look at his notes and maybe look up at various riders while he decides who gets what place. This is where you really need to hold your best WTB position until after the ring steward turns in the judge's card to the announcer. Good luck!

CHAPTER 6

———◄●►———

"Power Steering" Classes

In reining, stock horse, Western riding and working cow horse classes, Primo's performance is judged while you cue him in a pattern of tests. Most of the patterns require an accurate use of markers. Many patterns are done at a lope. The less obvious your cues, and the more accurate the patterns, the higher Primo's score will be. So I call these the power steering classes.

The conformation for an ideal reining horse is a good standard for any Western performance horse. He needs good, sound legs (feet included) that can hold up under stress. He needs a long, sloping shoulder, short back, strong loins and long hips. (The slope of his shoulder should equal the slope of his hip.) He should carry his head at wither level or a little higher. It helps, of course, if the horse is attractive. A pretty head catches the judge's eye. As for attitude, look for a quiet, relaxed horse who wants to please his rider. After all, the biggest part of any good performance horse's talent is in how he thinks and tries. As some horsemen say, "It's all between his ears."

A *stock horse* in the Arabian division means a reining horse.

Both the Arabian stock horse and the Quarter (Paint, Appaloosa or other) reining horse do the same patterns. The difference is that a stock horse is ridden more collected, with more rein contact. This changes his topline. He carries his neck a little higher and more arched. Many equitation riders like a stock horse because of his smooth way of doing a reining pattern or rail work. This makes it easy for the rider to hold his or her attractive position. But any good mover with a good attitude can make a good rider look great, and vice versa. So I'll no longer point out differences between the reining horse and the stock horse. I'll call them both reining horses.

Strategy

Strategy is very important. More winning patterns happen because of careful preplanning (thinking the ride through) than because of the horse's ability or the rider's talent. Concentrate, therefore, on a smooth and accurate pattern. Start slowly. It's easier to speed up than slow down. Besides, a judge would rather see a smooth pattern done slowly than a fast pattern that's full of faults.

When schooling, avoid using patterns. School the *parts* of patterns, for example, circles, spins and stops. Change your routine. Don't practice every single move each time you ride. Keep Primo wondering what you've planned next. That way, he'll listen to you.

Here are some more ideas for showing strategy:

- Look at the arena's size. It will probably be very different from where you and Primo practice, so plan to adjust your pattern to fit it.

- In Chapter 1 we talked about the importance of ground surface. Check the arena's surface. An ideal reining surface is firm dry ground with 2 to 3 inches of soft topping (dirt, sand or shavings). Be careful of deep, heavy (cuppy) footing or ground that's too wet. If that's the condition of the arena, plan to go slower. It's better to have Primo's slide shorter than to have his feet skid out from under him!

- Warm up just enough to get Primo limbered up and let him know what's coming. You want him to look forward to a chance to show off. You don't want to wear him out or push him into thinking, Oh, no, not this stuff again! If possible, time your warm-up so you'll finish with just one or two horses to go. This puts Primo at his best and also gives you time to watch some other riders and see how they handle circles. If they're having trouble, the arena may be smaller than it looks. Ride accordingly.

- The shape of your pattern is as important as doing all the moves in their right order. This means having nice round circles, using the markers properly, using the arena center point and the like.

- If you make a mistake, forget it for now. Put your mind on finishing the pattern as accurately as possible.

Moves

Primo might have learned his reining moves by any of several different methods. This depends on who his trainer was. It also depends on how Primo responded as a green horse. Horses are thinking individuals, not machines. They vary in how fast they learn different things. They vary in how (and where) they like to be cued. This chapter goes by the same basic horse/rider moves and cues that I've already explained. But a reining horse does his patterns much faster than a trail horse. Maybe that's why Craig Johnson, a world champion trainer and rider of reining horses, said what he did after reading the first draft of this chapter. He told me that he does some things differently from the way I tell you to do them, but he didn't say that my ways were wrong. Because Craig is a great trainer, I felt it important to include some of his comments in my explanation of how to ride a *finished* horse.

Joe Hayes, another world-class trainer of reining horses, lives next door to Craig. I've included some of Joe's ideas, too. For example, Joe says he always has a vet pull a colt's wolf teeth and float his molars before starting the colt on a bit. This simple procedure eliminates one possible problem, a sore mouth, before it can get started. Even though Primo is already on the bit, you should have a vet check his teeth.

Leg Yielding

Leg yielding means that Primo yields to pressure from your leg by moving away from it. He leg yields for you to open his side doors for turning on the foreleg, turning on the haunches and sidepassing. You can also use leg yielding for turns, controlling his circles, changing his leads, two-tracking, holding him in a countercanter and other moves. Leg yields are usually but not always teamed with rein cues.

Circles

Primo needs good lateral flexibility (the ability to bend) to make smaller circles, but he should travel straight for any circle that's large enough to require him to move forward. *Straight* here means that his back feet follow (track) his front feet. It's the opposite of going crooked. It has nothing to do with the shape of his pattern, which could be a straight line, a circle or a turn.

Use your regular cues to get Primo loping in a circle. As Joe says, "Think of steering his *shoulders* as well as his head." Once you've shown Primo the size circle you want, relax your reins (in gear, 2 to 3 inches of slack) and control him with your legs and weight. If he goes out of the pattern, immediately use the reins to correct him. Then release him again. You want to make Primo understand that he has to stay on the same circle pattern you put him on. Don't let him constantly rely on your reins as his guides.

If Primo slows down, speed him up by driving him with your legs. For even more speed, lean more forward. If he swings outside (or inside) while doing his circles, move him over with your leg. He should respond promptly. If not, you need to work on leg yields before continuing to school on circles or other reining moves.

A total of fifteen minutes of daily schooling on circles in each direction is usually enough. Divide the time period into several sessions, and do something else other than circles in between. You can ruin a horse by circling him too much. Most of your circles should be large, maybe 60 feet across. When a horse is overworked on small circles, he tries to rest his back by angling his hindquarters to the outside. (He allows them to surrender to centrifugal force.) This causes him to step outside in back, to "fishtail." As his outside hind foot steps wide of the circle, the extra strain on his inside front foot makes him drop his inside shoulder. When Primo drops his inside shoulder, it throws him off balance. He no longer travels straight. He goes crooked. You can help him without using the reins. Slow him by straightening, then shift your shoulders slightly to the outside in a "flamingo" exercise. However, if Primo is going crooked because he is tired, maybe even sore, you shouldn't keep on circling him.

If you're in a rectangular arena or a big field, and you're schooling Primo on gaits or just exercising him, school him also in six-or eight-sided figures or D-shaped patterns to keep him listening. But the circles he makes as part of a reining pattern should be nice and round, not oval or some other shape. Whether they're large or small, Primo's circles should end where they begin.

Find clean ground (without prints). You'll use it to record his hoofprint pattern to study later. For now, stay balanced and *look where you want Primo to go.* Have your overall pattern already clear in your mind, and look ahead. This also applies to following a straight line or any other pattern. But for making a circle, keep your eyes set on a point about a quarter circle ahead. You can't do that and also lean down to see how his pattern is shaped.

Start circling at a marker so you'll know when you've made one complete circle. As soon as you've come back around to the marker, take a couple of strides to start a second circle on top of the first. Then turn out of the circle and stop so you can read the footprints.

You can tell which prints are from his front feet because they are rounder than back footprints. In the circle, Primo's prints should meet end-to-beginning. If a video is made of Primo circling, it should be from a bird's-eye view as well as from a judge's viewpoint. The bird's-eye view would show details about Primo's body and yours while he circles, and it's always helpful to see how you look from where the judge sits. (For reining classes, the judge sits at the center of a long side.) If you don't have a camcorder, find a helper with a good eye for details.

Whenever you feel that Primo has made a really nice circle (or has definitely shown improvement), reward him with praise. Then go on to something else, something he likes. This shows Primo he's done what you want and keeps him eager to please you.

Leads

Simple Change of Leads

A *simple change of leads* is done by breaking from the canter to the walk or trot, taking a few strides at this new gait, then cantering again on the opposite lead. Several tests ask you for a simple change of leads. You might do it along a straight line, at the center of a figure eight or while riding a serpentine pattern between markers.

I'll explain how you'd change from the left lead to the right lead. Just reverse everything for changing from a right to a left lead. First, canter to the left on the left lead. Break to the walk or trot and take a few steps to be sure Primo is straight from head to tail. Then ask for a canter departure on the right lead. Follow the instructions in Chapter 5 for making transitions to a canter. Remember: don't ask Primo to turn until he's cantering on the new lead.

Flying Change of Leads

The *flying change of leads* is done with no interruption of the canter. In other words, you don't slow down to the walk or trot before switching leads. Otherwise, you use the same weight, leg and rein signals to ask for a new lead. Problems in making flying lead changes usually come from the rider's timing of aids, not from the horse himself.

The only time Primo can make a flying change of leads is during his period of suspension. The period of suspension is when all four of Primo's feet are off the ground. It happens right after the pull. Therefore, ask him while his leading leg is on the ground and pulling. That way, when that front leg finishes its pull and leaves the ground (having passed backward under Primo's shoulder), he can immediately arrange to push off with the new back leg when that back leg lands.

The best moment to ask for a flying change of leads will vary slightly from horse to horse. But it always occurs sometime between when the original leading foot hits the ground and when it leaves the ground again. (As you can see, we're talking about a very brief moment in time.)

Do not begin to turn Primo in the direction of the new lead before the actual lead change has occurred, the same as for the simple lead change. Sometimes, when watching a good reining horse change leads across the center of a figure eight, you may think the rider turned the horse at the same time he asked the lead change. Not so. It all just happened so fast that you missed it. *You must change leads before changing directions.* The only exception to this rule is when you're asking for the countercanter, to be discussed later in this chapter.

Sometimes you need to ask for a flying lead change when Primo is moving fast and you need to take a two-point position to keep up with his CB. In this case, you'll ask for the change from a standing position. Use your leg cues in the usual manner. But also drop more weight into present your inside stirrup (your right stirrup for a change to the left lead, left stirrup for change to the right lead). Simply stand a little harder in your inside stirrup as you move your outside leg slightly forward to ask for the new lead.

Be careful not to weight this inside stirrup before you ask for a change with your opposite leg. If Primo begins shifting in response to your use of weight before you open the other door, he'll either have a poor change or none at all.

You probably need more practice with markers than Primo does. Besides, if he's been around a while, he's smart enough to recognize markers as meaning he's supposed to do something. He may try to outguess what you want him to do instead of listening to you. This is where dressage letters can come in handy. You can use them to school yourself at using markers without Primo responding to them. You can use the letters any way you please and make up your own patterns. Of course, sometimes you need markers inside the arena for schooling Primo.

Common Lead Problems

Maybe this can help you recognize problems and correct them:

Problem #1: Primo won't change leads at all.

Explanation A: He can't change leads if he's crooked or too strung out to be able to respond soon enough to your cues. Straighten him or collect him more. Then ask him again for a lead change.

Explanation B: You turned him before he could change leads. Your timing was off. Learn where his feet are.

Explanation C: You didn't use your leg cues properly. Learn how your leg and weight cues work.

Explanation D: You didn't cue strong enough or soon enough for Primo to feel it and respond. Work on strengthening your legs and back.

Problem #2: He changes leads in front but not in back.

Explanation: This is the "push-over-pull" cross-canter (disunited canter). Most likely your timing was off for asking for the switch. Primo couldn't change leads in back because his other back foot was already weighted down on the ground. Sometimes it's not your fault and it happens because Primo either gets confused or lazy. He drops his shoulder to the new direction before he changes his back lead.

Problem #3: Primo responds to one lead but often misses the other.

Explanation A: Usually this is the rider's fault, and usually the right lead is the bad side. Most riders are right-handed. If they have problems, evidently they're right-legged also. Most missed-lead problems can be identified by watching a video in slow motion. It will show the rider contacting the horse with the right leg or foot (or seatbone). Sometimes you'll see this done in addition to giving correct cues with the left leg. Perhaps a rider will squeeze with the right leg for balance before cueing with the left leg. Perhaps he or she will ask for speed with the right leg / foot before cueing with the left leg. Surprisingly, most riders never feel themselves making these mistakes. However, once they've been shown what they are doing wrong, they can correct it.

Explanation B: Sometimes it's not the rider's fault. It's because the horse strongly favors one side over the other. Push him into the weaker lead (maybe use a corner) every chance you get. Make him develop that side, too.

Explanation C: The horse could be favoring a sore leg. Ask your farrier and / or vet about this possibility.

Problem #4: Primo makes the correct change of leads, front and back, but then he speeds up without being asked (and thereby loses points).

Explanation: This usually happens because of too much drill over too short a time, or because Primo gets excited if he hasn't had *enough* practice in making lead changes.

Frequent missed leads (also one-sidedness) can also occur if a rider has a slight curvature of the spine or an old hip injury. Although the rider is unaware of sitting off-center, the horse feels and responds to off-balance signals. This condition is similar to what happens to a rider whose legs are different lengths. That problem is solved by custom-measured stirrups. Off-centered problems can be corrected or improved by your awareness of them.

The Rollback

The *rollback* is designed to save time, ground or both. The cutting horse, or any working stock horse, cannot get along without this movement. Neither can the polo pony. It should be done as a continuous movement with Primo never completely halting during any part. Doing a rollback is the only case where Primo is allowed to lift his front legs off the ground (to rear slightly, in other words) for doing a turn on the haunches.

Here are all the parts of a rollback for you to put into one continuous movement: Canter into the rollback on one lead, put on the brakes, push off, then depart on the opposite lead. For example, you'll canter in on Primo's left lead, push off the left front foot, do a half-circle turn to the right (pivot around his right rear leg), then head out on his right lead. I'll assume Primo has already been taught how to do the rollback. And I'll show you how to ride it.

Just as you arrive at a marker, brace with your legs to drive Primo's legs under him, then use your weight and reins to stop him. Now, let's describe a rollback to the right.

You've passed the marker and Primo's back legs have stopped, but there is still some forward motion to his body. Place your left leg where you normally do to ask for a turn on the haunches and push hard on your left stirrup. Neck-rein to the right, easing up on the rein when Primo gets halfway through his turn. This cues him to turn right. It also shifts your weight to the right. Your right foot, meanwhile, "points" where you want to go. It bears very little weight. Think of yourself as actually beginning to go through the motions of doing a rollback all by yourself. Primo will join you. When he feels your weight shift to the right, he'll move under you to balance himself. Both of you are helped along by the momentum of barely stopping after moving fast. Throughout the rollback, *look* in the direction you want Primo to go. Your eye control is very important. It guides both you and Primo through this move. (*Note:* when Primo does a rollback while cutting, most of the time he'll do it on his own to follow the cow. He'll do what cutting people call turnabouts. This move differs from the turn*around* described for trail class and, of course, from the spin that some reiners call a turnaround. In cutting, the term turn*about* describes rollback-and-forths—meaning that Primo starts a rollback in one direction, then quickly shifts to start a rollback in the other direction in order to keep facing the cow. In other words, he usually does not actually complete the rollback to head back in the other direction. As his rider, you'll watch the cow and be set to go with Primo. Rather than cue Primo, you'll more likely just keep up with him.)

Balance your weight evenly again when the turn is about to be completed. Have your weight divided equally between your two stirrups by the time Primo is ready to canter away. Reverse your signals for a rollback to the left. And don't forget to praise Primo (during practice, anyway).

Now, here are some tips:

- Know where Primo's feet are before asking him to turn. The back leg he'll pivot on should be in front of, not behind, the other back leg. If his legs are out of position, his turn will be a clumsy walk-around, which he'd probably do only after you really pulled him around with your reins. It might help, during schooling, to back Primo a few steps before turning him. That way, he'll already have his weight shifted more onto his haunches. It'll also be easier for you to feel where each back foot is. (When Primo backs, his feet follow the same diagonal X pattern they do for a trot.)
- Even though it's a continuous motion, don't ask him to turn while he's still moving forward. This can strain or injure his legs. Learn to feel the difference between Primo not traveling with his back legs and Primo being totally stopped. Turn him when you're between those two stages.
- Primo's head and neck are elevated and his entire frame is shortened as the turn begins. It will stay that way until the turn is at least half completed. At that

point, Primo will stretch his neck for cantering out of the rollback. Be ready for this and follow with your hands. Don't jab him. It's not much of a reward for doing a good job!

The Pivot (or Offset)

The only difference between the *pivot* and a regular turn on the haunches is how fast the turn is performed. A pivot is done fast to show Primo's lightness and ability to respond quickly to your aids. A quarter-or half-circle turn is usually what is asked for. A pivot differs from the rollback in that it's always done from the halt. Also, Primo elevates his forehand as he gets ready to do the pivot. But he only does it to lighten his front end. He'll shift his weight rearward, rocking back on his hocks. He should not turn by rearing and throwing his weight to the side. Done properly, he uses his forelegs to stroke around to the side, pivoting around that side's back leg. As he turns, one or sometimes both forefeet will be in contact with the ground. (See "Turn on the Haunches" in Chapter 4.)

Before asking for a pivot, stop Primo when the leg he'll pivot on is due to land. As you stop, use your leg on the pivoting side to urge that back leg further up under Primo. Then immediately use your leg on the opposite side *plus* a neck rein to ask Primo to turn on his haunches. Alternate pressure-release with the neck rein instead of using steady pressure. This keeps Primo light in his turn. For two-handed reining, use an open or direct rein to turn him, supported by an indirect rein. Both you and Primo should look in the direction you turn.

The Spin

Like the pivot, the *spin* is a flat exercise. In other words, Primo does not rear with his front feet (lift them both at the same time, as he does for the rollback) in order to turn. The spin and the pivot are performed the same way except that the spin makes one or more complete turns. You cannot tell one from the other by looking at a photograph, but you can tell by viewing a video. You have to see the motion to tell how far the action goes. To perform the spin from the halt, do a pivot but continue it beyond a half turn. Keep pivoting until you've done at least one full turn on the haunches.

Practicing the spin is fun for you. But, for Primo's sake, don't overdo it. It's better to do several slow spins (basically at a fast walk) in good form than to go for speed and have Primo take bad shortcuts. He might rear and throw himself around, or else get tired and injure himself. Two or three spins in either direction are enough. Spins are like circles. You should do something else that's fun after Primo has done well. It's his best reward.

Backing

Backing was covered in Chapter 4, so you might want to reread pages 95 to 97. The basic commands are the same for asking Primo to start backing, to keep him backing and to stop his backing. But there is one important difference. Speed. To perform trail maneuvers without hitting a marker, each step back is done slowly. In reining, Primo will be asked to back more quickly. Also, he'll be expected to back straight for everything except trail moves.

The Sliding Stop

The *sliding stop* is merely a fast transition from the gallop to the halt. Before we discuss how to ask Primo for a sliding stop, let's first consider feet and footing.

Primo doesn't absolutely have to wear sliding plates (special shoes that are extra wide and smooth on the bottom) on his back feet to perform the sliding stop. Regular horseshoes will do, especially if he needs good rear-end traction for performing other activities. But if he's a serious reiner, he will need "sliders." In addition to special shoes for helping his feet slide, his legs should be wrapped for protection. The ideal surface has already been described on page 150. Be careful and go slow on hard ground or on topping that is too deep, contains rocks or is sloppy wet. Otherwise, you are inviting injury.

It's very important that Primo be straight from head to tail to perform a sliding stop. He must gallop forward in a straight line, then remain straight as he slides and stops.

Here's one way to produce a sliding stop:

1. Set up for your straight run by asking for a canter departure in the normal manner. Then ask Primo to tighten his canter into a concentrated mass of energy. You do this by urging him faster with your legs, but holding him back with your hands.
2. Next, allow him to stretch his head and neck, to lengthen his entire frame and shift his weight forward. Lean forward slightly and move your hand forward just enough to get him into a fast, forward-balanced canter.
3. Keep building speed. To do this, assume a two-point

position and lean forward. This shifts your weight / CB forward. Primo will go faster by shifting his CB / weight up under yours. Move your rein hand forward. Cluck for more speed. (These first three steps probably happen much faster than you can read about them.)

4. Now, just as Primo reaches his top speed for these conditions, you'll ask for the sliding stop. Pick the moment when Primo is stretched out in the "pull" part of his stride to ask it. That's when both of his hind feet will be off the ground. He can immediately respond to your signal and halt by shoving both back legs under his body. Use your regular stopping aids in the normal sequence. You'll sit, say "Whoa" and brace with your hands and legs. As Primo slides, you should be sitting straight, not forward or back.

Here are some more tips:

• Keep your weight centered in the saddle as you begin to drop your seatbones and brace your back. Keep your head up and look straight ahead. Keep your off hand relaxed and ready to push the saddle if necessary. You may need this help to keep yourself balanced upright when Primo suddenly shifts his weight to the rear.

• When you brace your legs on Primo's sides, be sure they apply equal pressure. This helps him bring his legs up under himself evenly. Your practice at riding without stirrups will now help you keep a good deep seat and a steady leg position throughout the slide. Try not to squeeze with your thighs or pinch with your knees. This pushes your seat out of the saddle and changes how you use your weight. However, it's better to squeeze than to lose your balance and interfere with Primo's efforts.

- After you've used your weight and said "Whoa," move your rein hand smoothly back to ask Primo to stop. As he obeys your direct rein action by setting his back feet to stop and slide, reward his obedience by releasing the rein tension. As the slide progresses, you might have a chance to check and release several times to make a longer slide. Releasing the rein tension during the slide also encourages Primo to walk ahead with his front feet as his rear feet continue to slide. You really get extra points for this!

There are two reasons why you want Primo to gallop prior to asking him to slide. First, the period when his back feet are off the ground is longer for the gallop than for any other gait. This gives you more time to use your stopping aids. Second, the faster Primo's speed is, coming into the stop, the longer he'll slide.

The Countercanter

In *countercanter*, Primo is asked to canter on the wrong lead on purpose. It is not a "push-over-pull" cross-canter. It follows the same "push-across-pull" footfall pattern as a regular canter. What makes it different is that Primo uses the outside lead for circling or turning.

Besides showing off Primo's advanced level of schooling, the countercanter serves two useful purposes. First, it trains him to be more coordinated laterally. Second, it makes him listen to you. He only uses the wrong lead because you ask him to. He wouldn't naturally do it.

When schooling the countercanter, keep your circles large and avoid sharp turns. Keep a steady balanced position. Don't lean or try to use your weight laterally. (In other words, don't play "flamingo.") Remember, Primo has to work harder to keep his balance on the outside lead.

One way to ask for the countercanter is to start a regular canter, then ease Primo into circling in the opposite direction without changing leads. Use your legs to keep him on his original lead and the reins to turn him in a countercircle. For

Sliding Stop
Several things that I've talked about in this book show up in this picture. You can see Arizona stretch his neck for counterbalance. His shoulders are lifted and his back is rounded. He's finishing the "a-cross" part of his gallop. His leading foreleg is about to "pull." Sarah is balanced perfectly in the saddle to feel Arizona's movement. When she sees his neck go down, she knows that it's time to say "Whoa" and lift the reins to begin their sliding stop.

Sliding Stop
Next she braces with her legs and pulls the reins slightly back. This picture shows how both horse and rider have to adjust their own weight/CB in order to change from a gallop (where weight/CB are shifted *forward* of midway) to a stop (where weight/CB must shift back behind midway).

example, use your right leg to ask for a left lead and canter several strides bending to the left. Keep cueing with your right leg and seatbone, but meanwhile guide Primo in a circle to the right with the reins, using one of two hands. Use your left leg just enough to keep him from drifting out. Or do a big figure eight. When you start your second circle, cue to change directions but not leads.

Two-Tracking

As you knew, in the *two-track* Primo's back legs move in a different set of tracks than his front legs. The easiest way for

Sliding Stop

As Arizona sits down and slides, Sarah sits nicely straight in the saddle . . . without using the horn or the reins to hold herself that way. Pictured here also are many details about how to ask for (and ride during) a great sliding stop. You can even use the telephone poles in the background to judge how straight Sarah sits. Notice that Sarah rides Arizona two-handed here. By the way, most of the horses in this book wear leg protection. Here Arizona wears bell boots in front (to protect his heels from being struck by his back hooves when he reaches under) plus a combination splint and ankle guard (for protection and support). In the two previous photographs you can see the skid boots that protect and support the ankles of his hind legs during the kind of action pictured here.

you to discover how to align yourself for doing the two-track is to ask Primo to do it alongside a fence. This is how he was taught, and it will also work for teaching you. At least it will work for the limited amount of two-tracking you'll do for Western riding.

Sliding Halt Asked For at the Wrong Moment
Look at Arizona's head and neck. Compare how he looks here with how relaxed he was throughout the stop shown on page 168. Here he appears tense. That's because Sarah asked him to stop when his head was coming up. Sarah's dad hasn't tried explaining footfall patterns to her yet. He simply tells her to ask for the sliding stop when her horse's head goes down.

Walk Primo in a straight line next to the fence. Keep him walking, and meanwhile use your outside leg and seatbone to move his haunches to the inside. Then continue to drive him forward with your legs. You may have to use the reins to keep his neck and head straight ahead. Cluck if needed, and use think-talk to keep him moving forward. That's it.

Western Riding

This is a contest for the reining horse to show that he can carry his rider around to do the usual ranch chores, take his

Maintaining a Countercanter

This is a great angle for you to see what both Sarah and Arizona do for a countercanter. They're circling around the photographer while he takes pictures. Arizona's feet and shoulders are correct for cantering to the right. Yet both his body and Sarah's cues are correct for cantering to the left . . . which is what he's doing, but on the right lead.

rider over trail obstacles and give a quiet, pleasant, comfortable ride in open country. The horse must prove he can do these things within a certain marked-off distance and in a given order.

Most rule books use the same pattern shown here. For that reason, you've got to keep Primo from anticipating. That's the number one concern with the Western riding horse.

The easiest way to keep Primo guessing is by not working on the routine pattern at home. School him as you would for any reining event. Go over all the basic moves every time you ride, but not in the same order. Trail-type lateral

Good Cues, Asking For a Lead Change
From this angle you can see Sarah's leg and two-handed rein cues as she asks Arizona to change from a left to a right lead. You can also tell how straight Arizona is. His back legs are nearly hidden behind his front legs.

exercises not used in reining or Western riding are good, too. They keep Primo flexible and listening to you.

Judges see more mistakes involving leads than anything else. Practice lead changes (simple and flying) every time you ride, making sure Primo has changed leads before you turn him. School him in a variety of speeds at the walk, trot and canter. Work on backing, circles, spins and sliding stops. Do some rollbacks. Make up patterns as you go along. Use your dressage letters instead of cones. As I mentioned before, this makes it harder for Primo to figure out what's coming up next. Or, go around two or three cones instead of all eight. Make a few circles at the countercanter. And remember to include some fun rides and road work outside

Lead Change, Period of Suspension
Three of Arizona's feet are clearly in the air. His weight is carried by his leading (left) foreleg. Sarah cues him to change to his right lead before either of his back feet touch ground. He *should* land first on his left back foot.

the arena. If you find a log while out on the trail, go over it several times. Circle a bush or a tree like it's a cone marker, then go over the log again. Take advantage of these natural obstacles and make it a fun game.

In other words, think like a horse and use your "horse" imagination to keep Primo listening to you and responding to your signals. This means you must listen to him, also. Maybe he's telling you his tack doesn't fit comfortably or his feet hurt. Maybe he's getting tired or bored. Maybe he

Lead Change Completed in Front Only

Arizona has made the change to the right in front, as Sarah asked, but he's still on the left lead in back. Arizona corrected himself on his next stride. Sarah didn't have to do anything extra before he changed. Meanwhile, we got a picture of a lead not changed in back. Most problems with leads happen to front feet, by the way, not back feet.

doesn't understand what you want him to do. It's only fair that you listen to your partner and treat him with respect.

The Working Cow Horse

The *working cow horse* is mentioned in this chapter because he does both rein work and cow work (cutting). Cutting is a performance specialty we'll talk about in Chapter 7.

The reining portion of this event is referred to as *dry work*. We've already covered this. A few horsemen believe dry

Sidepass
I asked Sarah to sidepass Arizona. This is not included in any reining pattern Sarah was used to doing. She had never sidepassed Arizona or any other horse before. Nevertheless, she followed my instructions —the same ones described in Chapter 4—and gave him the cues. And here is Arizona, obediently sidepassing to the right.

work is a waste of time. According to them, working the cow makes much more sense to the horse. But Craig Johnson says, "Those horsemen are ignorant. Never downplay the importance of having your horse broke."

Because I'm far more familiar with horses than with cows, I leave most of the decisions dealing with "cow psychology" up to my horse. Although we'll cover some points about

Spin to the Left

From this angle you can see Sarah's left rein opening one door and her left leg (heel) keeping another door closed.

Spin Continued

Now she's using both reins—a leading left rein and a right rein that's a strong indirect or maybe a neck rein.

Spin Continued, Now Second Time Around
This almost looks like how the spin started, but it's not. Arizona's really moving! Look at the strap away from his right side! Now that Arizona is doing what Sarah asked, she rewards him by lifting off her right leg and softening her rein cues. But she keeps clucking and driving him with her seatbones. He'll do another three spins and then she'll ease up on her cues and calmly walk him out to the left.

cutting in the next chapter, I heartily recommend that you do as I do. Leave most of the cow work up to Primo. Don't interfere any more than you have to.

Throughout this book I've stressed the importance of riding a finished performance horse rather than a green one. In this case, it's even more important because you need to be sure Primo *likes* cows before you go in the same arena with them. Some horses are afraid of cows. It's no fun being on the back of a big terrified animal, fenced in with other big animals (with sharp horns). That's when the arena will seem very small and crowded!

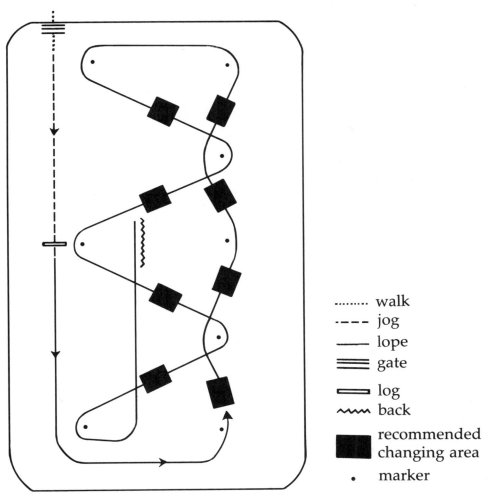

Western Riding Pattern

....	walk
- - - -	jog
————	lope
≡≡≡	gate
⊏⊐	log
∿∿∿	back
■	recommended changing area
•	marker

The dry work is done first. For shows that use two arenas, you'll do first one and then the other individually. But usually everybody is judged on dry work before the show staff clears all the markers out of the arena and brings the cows in. Then you have two minutes to work your cow.

First you and Primo go into a herd, where you pick a cow (it could also be a steer) for Primo to cut out. With Primo doing most of the work, you direct this cow to the fence.

Then you make it run down the fence line, turn it and make it run back in the other direction alongside the fence. As soon as you've gone far enough to prove to the judge that Primo has control of the cow alongside the fence, you urge the cow off the fence and put it out in the middle of the arena. Then you make it turn a complete circle in each direction.

Unexpected things can happen in this event. Much depends on what kind of cows are available for the event. Ideally, a cow will turn as soon as the horse closes in on it and starts to make the turn. If you draw a bad cow, Primo really has to work to earn his oats, not to mention his award! Read your rule book to see what he is allowed to do to make that cow obey and what will cause him to lose points. Then read Chapter 7 for more information about cutting.

CHAPTER 7

———◆◆◆———

Riding a
Cutting Horse

This will be a short chapter, because cutting is a specialty sport. Most youngsters under fourteen years of age who are active cutters got started early because one or more older members of the family were already involved. These youngsters learned to ride cutting horses and to work cows more by supervised experience than by reading. (However, you *can* learn a lot about cutting by reading and thinking.)

Cutting is not a sport for novice riders or, as a rule, for young riders. In the chapter on reining, you saw Sarah Johnson, only eight years old, have no trouble staying seated as her horse performed reining maneuvers, which included a very impressive sliding stop. But there's one big difference between reining maneuvers and cutting: Cutting uses cows.

For reining (also barrel racing and most performance activities performed by youth), the rider signals the horse what to do. But for cutting (also roping), cattle are added. When that happens, your horse will react as much (or more) to what the cows do than he will to your signals. That's why I consider most eight-year-olds too young to ride a cutting horse working cattle. I will explain how younger riders can learn to ride a cutting horse doing his moves without using cattle, however. And a twelve-year-old who rides well should be able to work "soft" (gentle) cows.

Although the cows do give an added element of danger, the sport of cutting is fun and fascinating. To me, it's sort of like playing chess on horseback. That's why I've included this chapter. Even though it's brief, it will give you an idea of what cutting is about, and get you started.

Primo's human trainer taught him the basics that any Western performance horse should know. Then the trainer gave Primo a few helpful hints on how he should position himself to be ready to move with the cow.

Perhaps I've oversimplified the trainer's job, but my point is this: In cutting, a lot of details are left for those cows and Primo to work out between themselves. Primo must think like a cow in order to be able to outthink it. Therefore you, as Primo's rider, must learn to think like a cow in order to be able to predict what Primo's about to do and to stay on him as he moves quickly to control the cow.

To keep up with Primo as he matches moves with the cow, you must have a secure seat and good balance. The hardest part about riding a cutting horse is keeping your seat. Cutters need to tuck and drive their seatbones into the saddle. The result, called a *cutter's slouch*, is not really a slouch. It's a deep seat, one that lets you "talk" and "listen" to Primo. It also gets your weight off his front end and lets you stay with him while performing extremely fast changes of direction. To achieve a deep seat, sit up straight and flex the muscles deep in your abdomen.

When Primo faces a cow, he'll switch back and forth on his haunches for doing turnabouts. When he does, keep your legs off his sides. (It's very important to keep your legs clear while riding a cutting horse who's working. Also, when you tuck your buttocks, remember to do so *without* changing leg pressure.) Stick your feet slightly out (rather than down, where they would contact Primo's sides) and push into one or both stirrups for counterbalance. Grab the horn and push against it, too. Flex your lower back and pelvis. Tuck your seatbones and use them for balance. Keep your shoulders level during his turnabouts.

I will start you out in a relatively easy situation. First, ask an expert to find you some nice calm ("soft") cattle. (Then expect to hear the expert's lecture on what breed of cattle are best for cutting. Most prefer Brahman crosses.) Anyway, ride Primo into the pen and head for the far corner while the cows are being let in. Stay in your corner while the cows mill around a while. Ordinarily, a rider will mix with the herd before the cuttings begin. This helps the cows settle down and get used to horses. It also gives you and Primo a chance to watch each cow. Some will be more active than others. You don't want the slowest cow. It probably won't move unless Primo gets rough. You don't want the most active cow yet, either. Pick a cow somewhere between those extremes. Try to find one that seems alert. Pick one that's watching you.

Primo will know that you want him to go after one of those cows. He'll be listening. In fact, he'll almost read your mind. Just point Primo toward the cow you want and pick up slightly on reins that otherwise will be very slack. Then set yourself squarely in that saddle and don't interfere. Be ready for anything from the cow and Primo.

Watch that cow. Learn to do what Primo does: "read" what that cow's about to do. That's the only way you can be ready to match your weight / CB with Primo's weight / CB when he moves to control the cow. Remember the things you learned in Chapter 1 about Primo's moves and how he balances? Well, now he's going to put some of those moves to a real test. And you won't necessarily be the one telling him what to do next. Most of the time, this is the cow's job. You'll discover that you had a distinct advantage when *you* were giving the orders. It gave you time to prepare yourself. You won't always have that time now . . . unless you become good at reading cows.

Spend some time working with this herd. Pick out a cow and move it away from the herd. Don't worry. Even though this is mainly Primo's show, you *are* allowed to step in and give a few orders. Just don't do any more guiding and cueing than you really need.

You can spend as long as you want on slow work, where Primo and / or the cow will take a step or two, then stand and stare at each other. But really fast work should only last twenty to forty seconds. When you're through working a cow, your signal for Primo to let her return to the herd is to pick up on the reins, or maybe back Primo up a step or two.

In *Ride Western Style* I explained how to use body language and think-talk instead of the lunge line to control Primo in a roundpen. Hopefully, you've read the book. If not, Primo himself has probably made you learn a few ways to stop and move horses without using a rope. My point is this: The more you know about how to use body language and think-talk instead of a rope to stop and move Primo, the more you will understand what goes on between Primo and the cow. In fact, it may help you more than reading an entire book devoted to riding the cutting horse. Primo's position relative to the cow works like your position relative to Primo when you're moving him with body language. Put him near the cow's hip to move the cow forward. Moving him to about midbody on the cow works like leg-yielding. It will move the cow over. Move Primo closer to the cow's shoulder to

Settling the Herd

Teresa approaches the herd on Miss Kitty so the cows can study the rider and especially the horse. If the cows don't move, she'll ease in closer. She needs to be able to circle and even enter the herd without scaring the cows into moving. These cows are relatively tame and accustomed to people on foot and to horses, but not to a horse and rider.

Studying the Herd

The cows are suspicious of riders. While waiting for Teresa to arrive at the Jones Ranch with her horse, I should have enlisted the Vestal children with their other horses to help me (riding Spot, behind Teresa) work on settling the herd.

turn it. And get him in front of the cow to stop and / or reverse it.

Like all animals (including people and horses), cows have certain invisible boundaries. Crossing the first boundary gets the cow's attention. Crossing the second boundary makes it move away. You'll want to stay right on, or slightly inside, that second boundary. There is a third boundary, one that can make a cow angry enough to fight back. Fortunately, you don't see fighting often when cows are in a herd. Generally they'd rather just stick together. You have to enter the herd and convince your chosen cow to leave. Then—and this is the most exciting part—you keep the cow from returning to the safety of the herd.

Add this information about cows to what you already know about riding. Play with the herd. However, don't overdo it. Cutting is a real workout for both Primo and the cows. This is why you only get two and a half minutes (two minutes flat for working cow pony class) to show what Primo can do during regular cutting competition.

It will take a while of playing with cattle to build your confidence. Then, when you're ready for more technical cutting information, I suggest two sources: a rule book and an expert on cutting. The expert help could be a book, a video, a coach, a clinic or a combination of these.

You don't have to use cows for practice. Goats and sheep will do fine. Some people prefer goats because they are faster than cows. This makes the horse work harder. Faster or not, goats and sheep have two big advantages over cows. They're cheaper to buy, and they cost less to maintain.

For that matter, you don't even need a live animal to practice some of Primo's moves. He can practice turnabouts by facing a "dummy" calf. This is a calf cutout rigged to ropes and controls. It can be made to move back and forth.

Holding the Cow, Helped by Turn-Back Riders

Teresa finally cuts one cow from the herd. Notice the slack reins and her hand on the horn for balance. This is so she won't interfere with Miss Kitty. The rest of us work at turning the cow back. We are in a big pasture, not a pen. *Warning:* Two very dangerous conditions are here. One is the presence of farm equipment. A cutting horse (or cow or rider) could concentrate entirely on the game and fail to notice the equipment until it was too late. Grass can be slick, especially when wet. A pasture is therefore not a good place for a cutting horse to perform. For that reason, Teresa plans *not* to let Miss Kitty show us several very fast and athletic cutting maneuvers that this mare enjoys doing.

Letting the Cow Go

Teresa doesn't feel comfortable about working this cow, so she uses the reins to tell Miss Kitty "Let this one go." Miss Kitty, however, doesn't want to quit. . . .

Staying On a Rearing Horse

Miss Kitty temporarily forgets her good manners. If Primo rears, do as Teresa does here. Lean forward, grip with your legs (mainly your thighs) and leave the reins slack. If you must hold onto something to keep from sliding down, grab Primo's mane. Do not use the reins. You might pull Primo over backward.

Backing Up as a Disciplinary Tool

This picture was taken right after Miss Kitty got excited. Teresa is using two of a rider's best disciplinary tools. She stays calm. And she firmly makes the mare back up. As soon as Miss Kitty starts backing willingly (a sign that she's ready to listen now), Teresa will stop backing and pick up wherever she left off when discipline was needed.

Doing a Turnabout

The cows refuse to cooperate. So, in order to get pictures, I let Miss Kitty "cut" *me*! Here she does a turnabout, in which the horse shifts back and forth on his haunches while facing the cow or whatever.

Doing a Turnabout

Here is another view of a turnabout, taken right after Miss Kitty has landed. She's in that "crossed-up" posture seen in many cutting horse pictures. Often, when facing a cow, the horse will "dive" right after the turnabout and snake out his or her head threateningly to block the cow. I'm trying to imitate a cow. Miss Kitty's expression says she isn't that easily fooled!

At the Show!
Smooth Eliminator is in the proper position to control the cow. Kyle stays centered in the saddle, not leaning to either side. Kyle's legs are relaxed and hanging loosely on Eliminator's sides, so that he doesn't inhibit the movements of his horse. (Photo: Teresa Jett)

Besides *what* Primo cuts, you must consider the surface he moves on and the surrounding conditions. Grass can be slippery footing, especially when it's wet. And when Primo is concentrating on the cow, he might not notice obstacles such as trees or farm machinery. Plan ahead. Avoid accidents.

The best way to find whatever animals you will practice on is to contact other people who ride cutting horses. They can also advise you on bits and other tack. Often they will meet at an arena regularly to practice. If the arena is large enough, and if there aren't too many riders, everybody stays in the arena. A few experienced riders position the cattle. The rest simply stay out of the way and watch until it's their turn. Usually you pay for each time you and Primo have a

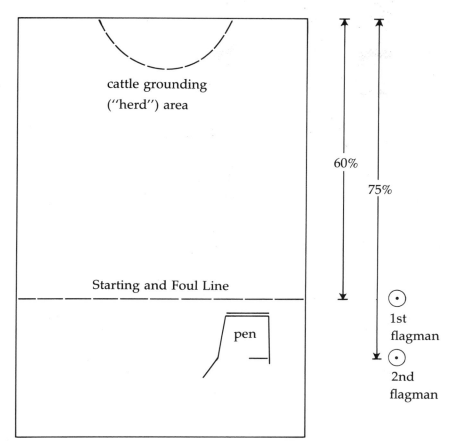

cattle grounding ("herd") area

60%

75%

Starting and Foul Line

pen

1st flagman

2nd flagman

Course Design for Team Penning

go against the cows. For example, you might pay $15 or $20 for five minutes. This might seem expensive, but it's worth it. A lot of effort goes into caring for cows and rotating new ones into the cutting herd. (After they have been worked a while, cattle tend to get "soured" on cutting and need replacing.)

By the way, both boys and girls can compete at cutting.

Team Penning

This newly recognized contest calls for a team of three riders. As with cutting, both boys and girls may compete. The team is assigned a number, but they don't know the number until the flagman announces it as a signal to start. The three riders have two minutes to do their job. Unless something unusual happens, rider 1 stays close to the herd, rider 2 stays about halfway (where some cows usually prefer to avoid the crowd, or herd), and rider 3 stays on the other side of the foul line. Rider 1 goes into the herd and finds which three cows wear the assigned number. These cows must be separated from the group and driven into a pen on the other side of the arena. Meanwhile, the team has to keep the other cows in the group from crossing the foul line. One popular strategy requires riders 1 and 2 to alternate with their duties. One turns escaping cows back toward the herd and meanwhile looks for another numbered cow within the herd. As soon as the retriever has a cow to the point where the third member can guide it into the pen, the retriever assumes turn-back duties. The riders are not allowed to touch or drive the cattle with their hands, hats, ropes or bats. All they can do is whistle and shout, slap their romals or reins against their chaps and use their horses to turn and drive the cows. The team getting their cows penned fastest wins.

As always, if you want to compete, read the rule book first. I can only cover the main points here. However, if you get the chance to work with cattle on a ranch, this chapter and the next one, in addition to what you've learned about Western riding in the rest of the book, should give enough information to get you started. Then you'll learn by doing. After all, experience is the best teacher.

CHAPTER 8

---◆━◉━◆---

Roping
Events

The roping horse and his rider work as a team in a two-sided game. You and Primo are on one side. The animal about to get roped is on the other. (For team roping, add the other rider and horse. Four of you team up against the steer.) Roping on the ranch is a matter of getting the job done any way you can. Roping in competition is something else. In addition to getting the job done, you must follow the game rules. Read your rules.

Both boys and girls can compete at team roping at most youth rodeos, but Little Britches and National High School allow only boys to compete in calf roping. Their rules committees think a calf is too heavy for most girls to throw down and tie. However, the girls have goat tying and breakaway roping. Other youth rodeos have exceptions to the general rule about whether boys or girls are permitted to do this or that. Mostly, it depends on where you live and who is in charge. Therefore, I can't say for sure who can do what. You will have to find out for yourself.

Various breed organizations, such as AQHA and APHA, also have roping events. At these horse shows, ropers are

193

expected to look good while they're doing their job. For example, Primo would get extra points for a nice sliding stop at a show, but doing that same stop at a rodeo would add unwanted time.

(*Note:* Much of the information here comes from what champion ropers Bobby Lewis and Robbie Schroeder said during a local horseman's clinic.)

Let's start by describing the ideal roping horse. Like the trail horse, he needs to listen to you and do what you ask, not do what he thinks is best. But he'll be a better, more dependable roping horse if he has "cow sense" (has a natural ability to work with cows). If you want to use the same horse for a lot of different activities, he can be any well-broke horse. If you're serious about roping, however, look for a horse with "cow" in his breeding. Look for a sturdy, well-built horse no bigger than 15 hands because it's easier for a horse of this size than for a long-legged one to match moves with a calf or steer. Also, it's easier to step down off a shorter horse. He's closer to the ground.

Equipment

The roping horse should have leg protection that's put on properly for a good fit. Otherwise, after getting hurt a couple of times, he won't want to work. Use bell boots to protect Primo's front heels from strikes by his back feet. Wrap his legs or use splint boots for protection and support. Use skid boots to protect his back heels. All this protection goes on just before you warm up. Remove it as soon as you finish riding.

Use *plain keg shoes* (or three-quarter ones) on his back feet. You don't want anything on his back shoes that could trip him. Use either keg or rimmed shoes on his front feet.

The roping saddle should fit low and close to Primo's back, with pads to make it fit even better. Fasten the front girth tight enough to keep the saddle from slipping. Fasten the back girth tight enough to keep the saddle from tipping up from the calf's weight on the rope. While not required, a breast collar is always a good precaution. Your stirrups should be short enough to brace you during your two-point position for throwing the rope and for stops.

There are two kinds of *horn wraps*. One goes around the saddle horn and acts as a shock absorber when you dally (wrap) the rope around the horn. Usually it's formed by wrapping several inch-wide bands cut from an old rubber tire tube. The other horn wrap is a harness that fits around the horns of a steer. It is used in team roping to protect the animal's head from getting rope burns.

It takes a while to adjust to your roping duties plus what you do to control Primo. During this period, a mechanical hackamore is the easiest and safest bridle to use. It gives you plenty of stopping power without damaging Primo's mouth. Whichever bridle you choose, the tie-down goes underneath it. Roping is one Western performance activity during which a tie-down usually helps Primo. It acts as a counterbalance to keep his head from going up or out too far when he stops. Don't tie him down too short. Adjust it so that when you lift the strap to remove slack, it will touch Primo's neck when he's relaxed.

A *neck rope* (or *strap*) is optional but handy. Adjust it to slide down Primo's neck 10 to 12 inches from his ears. It acts like a safety net for the rope, which passes through. You can use a neck rope to grab onto Primo rather than using the reins or something else that shouldn't be pulled on.

A *keeper* is handy for schooling, but not legal for some competition. There are several styles of keepers, mainly homemade. A small sturdy string or leather loop about the same size as Primo's hoof would do nicely. Loop it through itself onto the noseband of the tie-down. The rein (on your reining side) and the rope go through it. The keeper helps keep Primo pointed straight at the calf after you've made your delivery (thrown the lasso).

Incidentally, a snap on your closed roper's rein is more convenient than a buckle for times when you need to change equipment on Primo's bridle or neck. Snaps on both ends of your rein are even better. They're safer, too. You can quickly unfasten Primo's reins if he gets tangled.

Now we come to ropes. Calf ropes start out about 30 feet long, but they can be cut shorter. Bobby and Robbie both recommend starting off with a rope that's ⅜ inch thick and relatively soft. It's light and easy to handle. You'd be less accurate and get tired sooner throwing a long, stiff, heavy rope. Besides, it will be a while before you'll want to try roping anything that's too big for a ⅜ rope to handle.

The *hondo* (or *honda*) is the eye at one end of a rope through which the other end is passed to form a running noose or lasso. It can be knotted, spliced, metal or plastic. You won't always want to throw a lasso that draws up tight. Mostly you'll want one you can slip off easily, perhaps without even needing to dismount. A breakaway hondo will separate automatically so that the noose is released. One popular style of breakaway hondo is an eye made of hard plastic. The eye is completely formed, but the top is split. When pressure is applied, the eye opens at the split and allows the rope to slip out. Or, you can keep the noose from tightening by making a knot that's too big to pass through the eye. For calf-roping practice, tie the knot about two feet down the rope from the hondo.

Another important rope is your *pigging string*. That's the

small rope you'll use for tying the calf's feet. This rope can vary from ¼ to ⅜ inch in diameter and is about 6 feet long. Both calf ropes and pigging strings vary in how tightly they're woven. Fibers that are tightly woven are hard and stiff, but strong. Looser weaves are more flexible.

Calf Roping and General Roping Information

All horses in roping events must start from in the *roping box*, located on either side of the chute. When you're backed into the box, looking out, the chute would be on your left for calf roping. For team roping, the heeler uses this box. The header backs into the box on the other side of the chute. In addition, there's a barrier (usually 10 feet away) that the calf crosses for its head start. At that moment, a flag is dropped and Primo can leave the box.

Primo's manners in this box are important. Ride him alongside the chute to enter the box so he sees the calf. Then back him into the corner farthest away from the chute. If the chute has some protective padding in the far corner, you can back him in snugly. Corner padding works like leg protection. It helps keep a roping horse happy about doing his job. From this corner Primo can see the calf break, then use the shortest path (a diagonal line) to chase it.

Don't always chase the calf after it breaks out. Let an occasional one go during practice. This keeps Primo listening for your orders. If he gets too excited to settle down and pay attention, find an expert to help you. There are too many different causes and cures for me to list them all here. A word of caution, however: Some cowboys still train by methods that are too rough by today's standards. Allow your common sense to tell you when it's best to say "No thanks" and look for a kinder cowboy to help you.

Getting Primo settled properly in the box is called *scoring*. You want to reach the calf as soon as possible after you leave the box. But Primo will lose points if he leaves the box too soon (meaning, before the calf gets its head start). School Primo to move on your signal, *not* when he hears the chute gate bang open or sees the calf run out.

After Primo gets you to the calf, he *rates* the calf by keeping you in the ideal position for throwing. He must keep you in that position no matter how the calf dodges or changes its speed. He's judged on how well he does this.

You alone can decide what position is best for you. It's like lining up with markers for trail and reining classes, except this marker is alive and moving. Some riders like to be close to the calf, with the horse's head almost touching its hip. Others want a bit more distance between them and the calf, as a precaution against getting tangled. Wherever your spot is, that's where Primo should put himself as soon as possible. And that's where he should stay until you throw your rope.

It will take a while for you to get your timing worked out. Rating a calf is very important, so you must teach Primo to do it well. You should work on getting the position right before you try to throw a rope. When you are first learning to rate, you might be better off not even carrying a rope. Concentrate on your riding and on keeping Primo where you want him. You don't even need to start out of the box. Just turn the calf (or goat or sheep) loose in the arena and follow it around. Practice keeping Primo's back parallel to the animal's back.

When you do throw the rope, it's a warning to Primo, not a signal to stop. As soon as your loop is over the calf's head, you must jerk the slack to keep the calf from running through the loop. You do this by *dallying* (wrapping) the rope around your horn. One dally is enough. Two dallies can get you into trouble.

Speaking of trouble, that's what you'll have if you don't learn how to handle the rope, particularly for making your dally around the horn. Always hold the rope with your hand *behind* it, so it's free to go when you open your fingers. Don't hold it where it has to pass over your hand. Keep your thumb up, or away from the horn, while you hold the dally. A thumb can get caught and pulled off. Have every other part of your hand flush, so nothing sticks out to get caught on. Hold the reins up high over Primo's neck so they won't interfere with the rope. (See the top photo on page 208.)

The moment the loop is jerked tight, throw the slack away. Throw it up in front of Primo. This serves two purposes. It keeps the slack from getting tangled up in your gear, and it's a part of your signal to Primo for the stop. It gets him ready. But he shouldn't actually stop until you put your rein hand on his neck and say "Whoa." By putting your rein hand on Primo's neck, you also leave the "neutral" rein signal there to stop.

Step off, don't vault off to dismount. You should already have your weight on the stirrup and your other leg over the saddle by the time Primo backs to take the slack out of the rope. Time your dismount with Primo's move back so the momentum will "send you down the rope" to the calf.

Next, Primo is judged on how he works the rope. You'll need an expert's help with this. Done properly, Primo keeps the rope taut but he doesn't pull the calf down. He always faces the calf and keeps its face slightly off the ground.

Of course, you have to catch the calf before Primo can work the rope. You need a coach to get you started on using a rope. Then you need lots and lots of roping practice!

Technique is the most important thing a good roper must

develop. You will also need plenty of strength and stamina. Both you and Primo must be very fit to rope calves. Think about what happens. You start Primo from zero to wide open in moments, followed by a hard stop. You swing a rope, throw it, hurl yourself off the saddle and run down the rope to the calf. Then you pick up, throw down and try to tie a highly uncooperative animal weighing anywhere from 100 to 400 pounds!

This definitely requires speed, strength and endurance. A weight-lifting program will increase your upper-body strength. Running will build your endurance. The best way to practice for the kind of speed you need is by sprinting in the arena, wearing boots. This will develop the muscles you really use. I urge you to concentrate on physical fitness. Any riders, but ropers in particular, who are in good condition get hurt less often. If they do get hurt, they recover more quickly.

You are allowed two chances to rope the calf if you carry two loops. After you've roped it fairly, gotten to it and thrown it down, you use your pigging string to tie it by crossing any three feet. Then you throw both hands in the air to stop the clock. The fastest time (provided the tie holds) wins.

This chapter gives you an introduction to calf roping. But I heartily recommend that you attend one of the many good roping schools around the country. Some schools and places where you can order videos are listed in Appendix 1. Roping adds a new dimension to riding. It's important to have an instructor point out mistakes and correct them before they become bad habits. Every aspect of roping is completely covered and you will get plenty of chances for practice runs. Most schools will videotape your practice sessions. You already know how valuable this can be. Usually there's a contest at the end of the session, with prizes. Finally, you'll find out what equipment you'll need for schooling back home. You can probably buy everything you need right at the school. Some schools even sell roping horses.

Breakaway Roping

Breakaway roping is a timed event with a two-minute time limit. It follows the same general rules as calf roping, except that a cloth or flag is attached to the end of the rope. The flag is loosely tied to the horn. After the calf is roped and reaches the end of its line, the flag breaks free. (That's how the event got its name.) The timer stops the clock when he or she sees the flag break free.

Dally Team Roping

As you know, *dally* means the wrap the cowboy makes around his saddle horn with the rope slack to hold the calf, steer or other animal. For humane reasons, calves are not used for team roping. Steers are because they are bigger. And their horns are wrapped.

Team roping requires a "heading" horse and his rider plus a "heeling" horse and his rider. It starts off just like regular calf roping and has a two-minute time limit. The main difference is that the steer is stopped by two ropes. The header throws the first rope over the steer's head. Then he takes a dally in the rope and uses the rope to turn the steer so the heeler can get his (or her) rope around its rear foot. After the heeling rope has the steer stretched out and both horses facing each other, the clock is stopped. The steer is not thrown and tied down.

A horse that has been used for calf roping would have no problem adjusting to being a header at team roping, and vice versa. But some horses have trouble adjusting how they rate from the heeling position to how they rate for the head.

Goat Tying

The time limit for goat tying is one minute. When the clock starts, each girl races her horse from the score line to a goat, 40 yards away. The goat is tied there by a 10-foot rope. She dismounts and throws the goat by hand. (Unusual roughness in handling the goat will disqualify the contestant.) She crosses and ties any three feet with a pigging string. Then she steps back 3 feet from the goat and throws both her hands in the air to stop the clock. If a contestant gets tangled with her goat and falls, however, the judge will not require that she step back before stopping the clock when the tie is finished. The tie must hold for 6 seconds. The fastest time (without being disqualified) wins.

More About Youth Rodeos

Since I've mentioned Little Britches and National High School rodeos several times, let me tell you something about these worthwhile organizations.

Little Britches is the largest and one of the oldest youth rodeo organizations in the United States. Junior members are ages eight through thirteen and senior members are fourteen through eighteen. Besides the roping events already described, they offer steer wrestling, bareback and saddle bronc riding, steer or bull riding, cloverleaf barrel racing, pole bending, flag racing, a trail course and goat tail tying (an event for junior girls in which the goat's tail is tied rather than three legs).

National High School rodeo is for students enrolled in the ninth through twelfth grade and under the age of twenty. It offers calf roping, bareback and saddle bronc riding, bull riding and steer wrestling for boys. Cutting horse and dally team roping events are for boys and girls. Girls have barrel racing, pole bending, breakaway roping, goat tying and a queen contest. Out of a total possible 250 points for the queen contest, only 50 points apply to horsemanship. The other points apply to the girl's looks and personality, her response during an interview, prepared and impromptu speeches plus taking a test on what's in the rule book.

Rope with Breakaway Hondo
This rope has a hard plastic breakaway hondo.

Properly Rigged for Roping
Ty holds his pigging string in his teeth. That's a good idea. Both hands are free for riding and roping, then his string is convenient for when he needs it fast to string the calf's feet before losing his grip. Ty carries an extra string tucked in his belt, in back. Rusty is suitably built and rigged for roping.

Rigged for Schooling

For schooling, the rope passes through Rusty's neck rope (or strap) and through the keeper on the tie-down's noseband. One end of the rope is dallied around the horn. Ty holds the reins up so you can see the equipment better.

Scoring

Terry releases a calf, but Ty lets it go and stays in the box. Ty does this sometimes during practice to keep Rusty paying attention to *him*, not the calf.

Rating

Rusty rates the calf while Ty prepares to throw the rope. Rusty has his weight forward. Notice Ty's seat.

Making the Catch

As the noose settles around the calf's neck, Ty leans forward and prepares to dally the rope. Feeling Ty's forward shift in weight, Rusty understands this cue to shift *his* weight back to stop himself and the calf.

Roping Horse Holding the Calf

Not knowing where the calf would run or when Ty would rope it, the photographer ended up too close to the action to get a picture of both Rusty and Ty. So here's Rusty calmly holding the calf while Ty's having a workout at the other end of the rope. I learned right afterwards that this was Ty's first time to rope and tie a calf!

Good Tie

Rusty's at one end of the rope. Here's the other end. Ty made a good legal tie on his first calf.

Header for Team Roping

As Terry's rope falls around the handsome Longhorn heifer's head, study the position of this expert rider and seasoned horse. Notice how Terry handles the rope so he won't get his hand caught. Terry's horse rates closer to the heifer than Rusty. That's where Terry wants him. Ty wants Rusty farther back because he prefers more room for aiming and delivering the rope.

Header Setting Up for Heeler

Terry maneuvers turns the heifer so Ty can try to get his rope around her back foot or feet. That one missed.

Good Catch by Heeler

This time Ty got her. As you can see, he's not yet dallied the rope around his horn.

Completed Head/Heel Catch

So. This heifer is properly headed and heeled.

CHAPTER 9

———◆◀●▶▶———

Timed Speed
Events

Barrel racing, pole bending, stake racing and flag racing are
called *timed speed events*. Horse and rider pass a score line to
start the clock, then work through a given pattern and hurry
back to the score line to stop the clock. The fastest ride wins.
Of these events, barrel racing is best known. Also called
cloverleaf barrel racing because of its cloverleaf-shaped pattern, it began in the mid-1940s in Texas. Pole bending and
the other races came along later.

Timed speed events are very popular at rodeos and Western horse shows. In addition, local clubs hold weekly jackpot
races in areas (in north Texas, for example) where barrel
racing is popular. Contestants pay an entry fee for each run.
Part of that fee goes to the club for operational expenses.
The rest of it goes into the purses, or prize money. The
winner receives the largest share, second place the next
largest, and so on through fourth place, depending on the
number of entries.

To do well at timed speed event, as with any other competition, you must be a good rider. You have to gallop Primo

toward special spots, control him through the turns, urge him even faster after he's circled the final obstacle . . . then stop him after he's crossed the finish line. You'll ride with both hands, using a short, closed "roper's" rein in a special way. You'll use a forward seat for speed, a deeper seat to turn and stop, and stirrups that are fairly short (just above your ankle bone) for leverage.

Before I talk about the particulars for each event, I'd like to mention some points that apply to them all.

- First, your horse must be sound (meaning healthy), responsive to your aids and flexible. He should also be fast. However, given a choice, choose obedience over speed. Any reasonably sound horse can run fast enough to win sometimes. After you've ridden long enough to have a better idea of what timed events are all about, then you can move up to a faster horse.
- You must work Primo into good shape and keep him there if you want him to do his best and be less likely to injure himself when he performs. This means riding him nearly every day. Ride long enough for him to break into a sweat. The more watery Primo's sweat is, the better shape he's in. A few "soapsuds" under the saddle and other places on Primo that get rubbed when he's ridden hard are normal. Otherwise, sweat that's thick and white shows he's working too hard for the condition he's in. Ease up. Have longer warm-ups and cool-downs. Do less galloping for a while, then gradually do more.
- *You* must be in good shape, too. What I said in Chapter 8 about a calf roper needing to be an athelete also applies to a speed event rider. A speed rider,

however, should work on being slim and strong. The fewer pounds Primo has to carry, the faster he can run. (That's why a barrel racing saddle is much lighter than most of the other kinds of stock-seat saddles. And incidentally, some overweight-but-talented riders *have* coaxed their horses around the cloverleaf pattern in winning times.)

- Both you and Primo should loosen your muscles and "wake up" your circulation before doing speed work. You both need a good warm-up and cool-down. Use a warm-up to get your minds as well as your bodies ready. Use a cool-down to reward your minds but mainly your bodies.

- It's just as important for Primo to have a daily turnout as it is for him to be ridden every day.

- You know to feed Primo right, groom him, take care of his feet and teeth, and keep him on a preventative health plan. But that's not all he needs. He needs to be comfortable while he rides in the trailer and when he stays overnight at shows. He needs comfortable tack. Check the fit of his tie-down, curb chain and bit. (When Primo stands relaxed, a properly adjusted tie-down strap can be lifted so that it will barely touch his neck.) Check his saddle and the padding under it, his girth, his breast collar and his leg wraps. Also make sure his sheet or blanket doesn't rub and irritate him.

- If you've gone through the check list and Primo still seems not quite right when he runs, maybe the trouble is with how you ride him. A video of your ride can help you here. However, Primo's problem could be that he's just tired and needs a vacation. Sometimes turning him out in a pasture to relax for a couple of weeks can do wonders.

Barrel Racing

In barrel racing you are allowed a running start. The clock starts when Primo's nose passes the flags (or, with electronic equipment, crosses the fixed beam). Three big (usually 40- or 55-gallon) barrels are arranged in a triangular pattern. The standard measurements shown in the diagram can be adjusted to fit into a smaller arena. It doesn't matter whether you start with the right or the left barrel, but most riders start with the right barrel. Once you start, you must complete the basic cloverleaf pattern. The pattern is one turn to the right and two turns to the left, or one turn to the left and two turns to the right.

Like roping, racing rules are more lenient about what Primo can wear than the rules of other performance classes described in this book. The object is to get the job done in a hurry, not to look pretty while it is being done. You may use whatever works best on Primo. This includes a tie-down and any kind of bridle rig, including a bosal or mechanical hackamore. Cruelty, of course, is never tolerated. The judge won't allow any equipment he considers too severe.

However, just because you're permitted extra equipment on Primo doesn't mean you should use it. Use the mildest and least that works. If you use a curb bit, be sure to select one with shanks that can swivel ("loose"). Primo's mouth would take a beating from your leading rein cues if the shanks were "fixed" (a solid part of the mouthpiece).

Schooling Without the Barrels

You don't run barrels quite the same way you ride in a pleasure class or an equitation class. You and Primo aren't judged on looks. You're judged on how long it takes him to

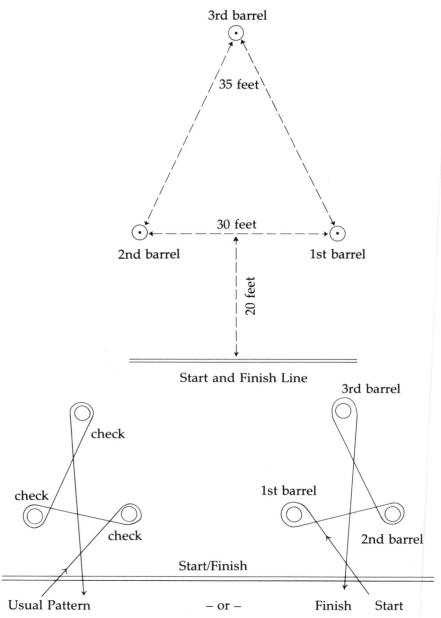

Barrel Racing Patterns and Suggested Dimensions

You may run a pattern starting with the left or the right barrel, but most riders start with the right barrel. These are the suggested dimensions. The barrels and Start/Finish line can be a little closer together if the arena is smaller, but keep the proportions similar to these here. For example, Start/Finish could be 15 feet instead of 20 feet, with 25 feet between barrels 1 and 2, then 30 feet each way to barrel 3.

complete the course without knocking down a barrel. Even so, *never ever* throw your equitation training out the window and ride Primo the way some people do, with heels kicking and arms flapping! Don't bounce around in the saddle or haul back on the reins, either.

As for Primo, although he'll be racing around as fast as he can, he *must* be a well-broke horse. He must respond quickly to your leg cue to move his hip or shoulder over. He must follow your leading rein. Otherwise, he'll knock down a barrel or go off pattern. If he doesn't take the proper lead and switch leads when asked, he won't be set up for taking the barrel in the first place. And if he doesn't stop when you ask him, you could have a wreck!

When you school Primo, work on his lead changes and his stops. Do this when you're out in the open as well as in an arena. Always insist on a "Whoa," but don't expect a sliding stop. It's more important for a barrel horse to have good traction for getting around the barrels and for running than it is for him to have a good slide. Rimmed shoes are good. Sliders are definitely out. Ask your farrier to show you the difference.

Include some exercises for flexibility. For example, while mounted and standing, you can use a leading rein to "ask for Primo's face." (That means getting him to bend his neck around so you can reach up and rub his face.) Don't pull him around. Patiently *ask* him with the rein and your voice. Practice doing this in both directions. Slow and fast spins in both directions are good for flexibility, too. So are rollbacks, figure eights, serpentines and corkscrews.

To do a corkscrew, start out by loping in a big circle. Let Primo move out and gallop at first if he wants to. It's better to let him work off steam now than to keep pulling on him. Besides, he's schooling for a speed event, not Western pleasure. After he's had his fun, he'll be more willing to listen when you need his attention. When you feel him relax through your hands and legs, it's time to start making the circles smaller. Finally, when he's down to a spin, let him walk or jog out of it. Go back to the big circle and repeat the exercise. Then circle in the other direction. Any exercise you do in one direction, be sure to repeat it in the other direction so Primo won't become one-sided.

You'll probably hear about some other exercises. Some are good. Some aren't so good. For example, if Primo is already flexible going around the barrels, he doesn't need a two-tracking exercise called the shoulder-in, shoulder-out. If this exercise isn't done right, or if it disagrees with your horse's natural way of turning a barrel (perhaps he sits down and slides around it, for example, this exercise can cause more problems than it can cure. Play it safe and stay with the exercises I've described.

Long reins are dangerous for barrel racing because they can get in the way. You'll ride with more rein contact because you'll need an immediate response from Primo. This is why I recommend a roper's rein. But because there's so little slack, when you bend Primo around a barrel with a leading (opening) rein, you really need to *give* (move your hand up) on the side opposite the bending side. After you've warmed up before the race, just sit there on Primo and slowly practice your "give-while-taking" reining motions. Remember, this is not an equitation class. Don't be afraid to move those hands! Keep enough room between your hands on the reins to have plenty of flexibility on either side of Primo.

Schooling on the Barrels

Any horse that uses a pattern during competition must be schooled on the moves he'll use. Unlike reining and Western riding, the barrel horse also must be schooled on the pattern itself. He needs to practice finding his pockets. A *pocket* is the actual path Primo should take to get around each barrel. You want him to "stay in his pocket."

There are two ways to approach barrels, but I recommend only one. If you're familiar with the game of bowling, you may recognize the terms "spot bowl" and "pin bowl." To pin bowl, you aim for the pins. To spot bowl, you aim for a set of markers (spots) on the alley. If the ball crosses the correct markers, it will automatically hit the pins you want. You've already used this "spot bowl" system. You've lined up markers for doing trail obstacles. Now think about barrel racing. *Aim for the pocket* ("spot"), not the barrel.

A pocket's size varies according to the horse's size and how flexible he is while getting around the barrel. But pockets have the same basic design. Those around the first two barrels are shaped like big fat raindrops. The barrel goes in the middle, toward the far side. The third pocket doesn't have a point to the raindrop because you'll head straight out of it and sprint to the finish.

The path you want Primo to take is the raindrop's outline. If he gets *inside* the outline or cuts it short, you risk hitting a barrel. If he gets *outside* the outline or cuts it deep, you waste valuable time. Also, getting off the outline can throw you off course for the next pocket. The O's in the diagram stand for tires or cones, markers that will help you stay in (actually *on*) the pocket. They're set up for starting on the right barrel. Switch the markers if you start on the left barrel.

When using barrels, school on checking Primo's speed just before he turns each barrel. This slowing down is also called *rating* by many barrel instructors. When you're racing, or when you're schooling *after you both have the pattern mastered*, this important step is barely noticeable. However,

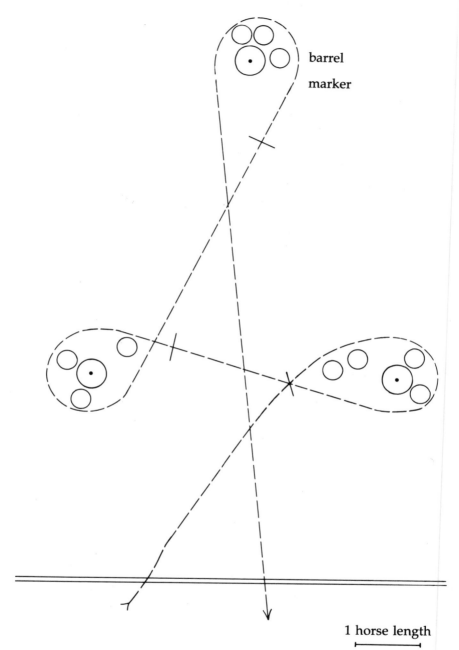

barrel

marker

1 horse length

Barrel Pattern with Markers

since it *is* so important, you should exaggerate it while learning. Exaggerate it by nearly stopping Primo (as for a rollback). If that doesn't get his attention, exaggerate it even more by making him stop and back a step or two before going around the barrel. Also exaggerate it to school Primo any time he forgets or needs to be fine-tuned.

Although Primo must master the cloverleaf pattern, he can get bored with it and start to make careless mistakes. Therefore, do some of your schooling around one barrel. Put it out in a pasture or another riding area instead of where the three barrels are set up in a pattern. While you school on something else, or while just exercising, slip in a few practice turns around the one barrel.

Before I take you through the pattern, let me make some additional suggestions now:

- Take the entire pattern first at a walk. Stop at each check point (X). Next, trot between barrels and walk around them. Then lope between barrels and trot around them. Finally, gallop between barrels and lope around them. *Never* speed up around the barrels.
- Modify the official pattern and school mainly by "no start, no finish." To do this, take your first two barrels as usual. After your third barrel, don't go back down the middle of the arena. Instead, finish your raindrop by heading for the outside rail (or some designated sideline point in an open field). Go slow for the turn and follow on around to the starting end. After you've passed the first barrel, turn in and start your pattern all over again. (You'll automatically be on the proper lead.)
- Any time Primo makes a mistake while going around a barrel (provided he hasn't knocked it down), go

around the same barrel again. Circle it two or even three times if necessary, but leave it and move on as soon as he improves. Any activity with your horse should end on a happy note.

Now, here's how to ride the pattern:

- First, get Primo warmed up and then settled down again before the race so he'll pay attention to you. Get off and check your tack. Stretch yourself nicely all over before remounting. Also hold your arms up and, with your wrists relaxed, shake your hands. Before you go to the alley, use your "give-take" rein exercise to flex and relax Primo. When you get to the alley to stand and wait your turn, stroke him. Some associations penalize you for no hat or helmet. Five seconds are added in AQHA rules if you don't keep your hat on for the entire run. A safety helmet is strongly recommended for speed events, so now is a good time to check your chin strap. Meanwhile, use this chance to look at the arena and think-talk every step of a perfect ride. Finally, take some deep, relaxing breaths and smile.
- Gallop to barrel 1 in a two-point forward position. (Some instructors call this a jockey position.) Aim for the inside edge of the pocket. It's located about one and a half horse-lengths (about 10 feet) before passing the barrel.
- When you reach the edge of your pocket, shift to a more upright seated position. With training, this change in your weight and seatbones should signal Primo to check his speed for the turn. Start then to push against your outside stirrup. When you consider Primo's speed and weight, you can see why you must

plan ahead. If you waited until his nose passed the barrel and his turn actually started, it would be too late. Keep your inside leg / foot close to the girth. That way, if Primo's hip or shoulder gets too close to the barrel, you can use your inside leg to move it off. If your inside foot sticks out, it will hit the barrel.

- As your foot pushes, turn Primo with a leading rein. *Don't wait until Primo's nose is even with the barrel to start turning him. "Take his nose" when he's still a body length away.* Practice is the only way to discover how high or how far out to hold the rein. If necessary, brace your other hand on the horn for balance and leverage. If you don't need your off hand for bracing, kindly "give" with it.

- Stop leading Primo around as soon as you've turned enough to line up with the edge of pocket 2. This requires looking ahead. As with reining or other fast moves, let your peripheral (side) vision and memory get you through the move you've basically finished. But focus on what's ahead.

- Take a two-point forward position for the run to barrel 2. Remember, aim for the pocket's edge.

- Shift to a more upright seat and push against your outside stirrup as soon as you enter the pocket. Change reining hands and start your turn. Keep your inside leg near the girth.

- Stop leading Primo around as soon as you can see a straight line from where you are to the edge of pocket 3.

- Move to a two-point position and keep Primo straight. You might need to use both hands to guide him.

- When you reach the edge of pocket 3, sit upright and follow the same instructions for getting around the barrel.

- As soon as your leg leaves the barrel, straighten Primo for his sprint to the finish. Take a more forward two-point position. This matches your weight / CB with Primo's weight / CB when he gallops hard. Move your arms as needed to follow his outstretched neck with the short rein, but hold your body steady and streamlined to help him go faster. Urge Primo with your voice. A voice that he trusts usually works much better than a bat or spurs.

- Get Primo across the finish line before you do anything about stopping him. Many a race has been lost at the finish line because the rider lacked confidence in getting the horse to stop after the finish line. So he or she started slowing the horse too early.

- As soon as Primo crosses the line, sit and brace your legs. Say "Whoa!" and use the reins to stop him. Be sure to use only as much pressure as needed. Use a series of pulls and releases rather than one hard pull. It's a good idea to brace yourself with one hand on the horn if Primo has a really good stop.

- After you exit the arena, reward Primo by praising him. *Never* discipline him if he knocked down a barrel or messed up in some other way. Besides, if a mistake were made, it was probably *your* fault, not Primo's. Act very calm. This works on yourself as well as on Primo. Ride him (somewhere out of the way of other riders) long enough for his breathing to settle before you get off. Loosen the girth after you dismount, even if you don't remove the saddle yet. Trade his bridle for a halter. These little attentions to Primo's comfort make barrel racing or any other performance activity more pleasant for him. They make him more willing to do his best.

Pole Bending

After your running start, the clock starts when Primo's nose crosses the line. You run straight to the far pole, round it and follow a serpentine pattern back between the six poles. Circle the sixth pole and zigzag back to the first pole. Go around that pole, then sprint straight back to the line to stop

Pole Bending Pattern

Like barrel racing, pole bending can start either from the left or right. Also, the distance between poles can be made a little shorter to fit into a smaller arena as long as the distances between poles and the Start/Finish line are equal.

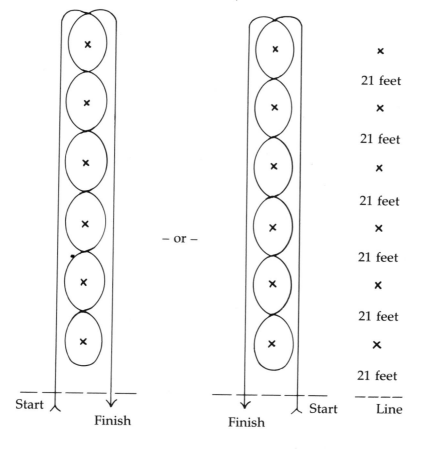

the clock. You may start from the right or left of the poles. But you must follow the stated pattern.

Similar riding and schooling rules apply to barrels and poles. You're penalized five seconds for knocking down a pole or barrel. You're disqualified for breaking the pattern. You'll turn Primo with a leading rein, check him by sitting, push off your stirrup and use a two-point for the sprints.

The poles in pole bending are supposed to be 21 feet apart in competition. But if the arena where you practice is too small for all six poles to be the full 21 feet apart, what do you do? Should you leave off one pole? Should you move the six poles closer together?

If Primo is used to the poles being 21 feet apart, he might automatically change leads on the same number of strides (every third stride, probably). His being automatic is good if you're learning the game because Primo can take you through the pattern. All you have to do is hold on. However, if you can't figure out what to do by studying the pattern in a book, then you shouldn't be racing around the poles! Changing leads automatically can lead to trouble if the footing and other parts of Primo's environment are not the same. Any changes in the footing can put Primo at a slightly different spot. The difference might not be much, but it's enough to make a difference. He'll be too close or too far from where he *should* be for a perfect run.

Therefore, it's better to shorten the distance (slightly and evenly) between poles in a small practice arena than to omit a pole. The same "signal" rule applies to pole bending and other timed speed events as for taking trail obstacles: Primo needs to listen to *you*, not just follow the pattern (even though he may know the pattern better than you do).

Now you know what to work on. Walk the entire pattern, then trot / walk, then lope/trot, then gallop/lope. Set a couple of poles out in a field so you can school Primo. If the field is used for turnout and / or other riding purposes besides schooling for speed events—for example, if someone is just learning to ride—do not charge through on Primo. Always be a good horseman and a good sport with other riders.

Stake Racing

The same general rules for a speed event also apply to stake racing. Start by crossing the center line between the markers, run a figure eight around the upright markers and finish by again crossing the center line. You may go right or left, just as long as you complete a figure eight. If you knock the marker down, you are disqualified.

Flag Race

Flag racing is mostly for younger riders. Popular in Little Britches rodeos, it's fun for both the riders and the spectators. Cross the start line (right or left) and run to the first barrel carrying a flag. Plant that flag in the first bucket, then go to the second bucket and take that flag. Carry it back to the line to stop the clock.

Other than losing time, you're not penalized for circling either barrel more than once. (Sometimes it takes a while to get Primo close enough for you to plant or grab the flag.) But you do lose two seconds for carrying the flag anywhere but in your hand. You're disqualified for knocking over the bucket or barrel, if the first flag falls out of the bucket, and for not carrying the second flag back across the line. You're also disqualified for using the flag as a whip.

Eligibility

More girls than boys ride timed speed events. Some associations only allow girls to compete, period. And some associations only allow girls to compete in national shows but boys may compete locally. So the rule is: It depends. Read the show flyers and the host association's rule book. Also check with any riders you know who have participated.

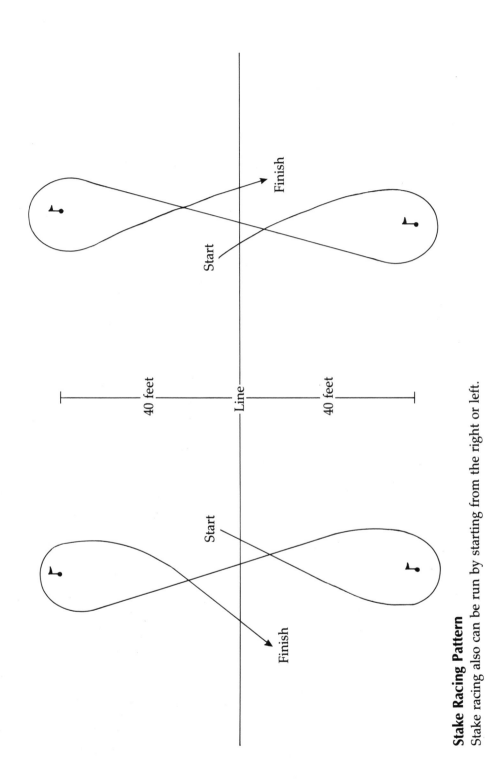

Stake Racing Pattern
Stake racing also can be run by starting from the right or left.

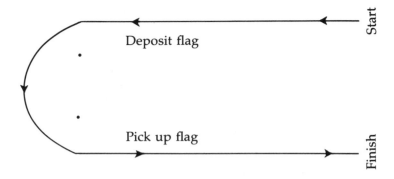

Start

Deposit flag

Pick up flag

Finish

Flag Racing Pattern

The barrels are 100 feet from the starting line and are placed no less than 25 feet apart.

Barrel Racing Champions

Kylie and her AQHA mare, Clark's Fan (Lady), show off the saddle they won. Carved on the fender is "Josey World Champion 1991 Barrel Racing Clinic."

Leg Protection for Horse and Rider

Lady's shin guards showed in the previous picture. Kylie wears shin
guards, too, in case Lady hits a barrel. Colliding with the rim,
especially, of a heavy metal barrel at high speed could badly bruise or
even break a rider's leg.

Horse and Rider Ready to Run Barrels

Here's the total picture, complete with my Western safety helmet (which nearly fits Kylie, by the way). The rein and bit are especially designed for barrel racing. The rein has little knots that help Kylie locate the best spot to put her hands (by feel) when she changes hands, going around the barrels. Martha Josey designed this combination bit and bosal. "Bit o' Bos" works best on barrel horses whose heads taper down to a fairly small size, like Lady's.

Going Around a Right Barrel (Indoors)

Going Around a Right Barrel (in Mud)

This photograph shows Kylie and Lady from a different angle than in the previous picture. Otherwise, both rider and horse use the same good technique, even though the riding conditions differ. In the first picture the barrel is on deep, dry sand, but it's indoors with shadows. Here, the outdoor arena has better lighting but muddy ground that's mainly sand (okay when wet) plus some clay (slick when wet).

A Crucial Moment for Every Barrel Racer

From this angle you can see how important it is to turn Primo at the right moment. Too soon will result in hitting the barrel. Too late will lose valuable time. Only by practice can you find how much "turn" to ask of Primo, and when to ask it. Another thing to mention: Keep your inside leg close to your horse's side. Otherwise you can hit the barrel with your foot. Kylie does a fine job here.

When to Assume a Two-Point Position

Lady has passed the barrel. Kylie assumes a two-point position and looks for the next barrel.

Leaving a Barrel

Kylie uses her weight and aids to help Lady bound away from the barrel and quickly pick up speed.

In Racing Position and Looking Ahead

Here's a good front view of Kylie in racing position and looking for what's ahead—either the next barrel or the Finish line.

CHAPTER 10

---◆◆◆---

Halter
Events

Halter classes are for registered animals only. The rules involve the horse's age, sex, show experience and other routine breed or color registration requirements. The rules don't tell how to show the horse. But "showmanship in halter" rules do give instructions because showmanship is considered a performance event. For showmanship, Primo may be registered, but it's not necessarily required. For example, 4-H and Pony Club horses don't have to be registered.

The biggest difference between halter and showmanship is this: Primo gets judged in halter classes for how *he* looks and acts while you handle him. You get judged in showmanship classes for how *you* look and act while you show him off. Although a large part of your score (40 out of a possible 100 points) applies to Primo's appearance, his conformation doesn't count. What does count is how well you've taken care of him and prepared him for this class. Therefore, this chapter concentrates on showmanship—the handling part. It doesn't cover grooming and management.

Your appearance can score 0 to 10 points. (The section on what to wear in Chapter 3 can help you here.) This leaves 0 to 50 points for how you handle Primo. Twenty of those 50 points apply to your poise and alertness. So don't let anybody or anything outside the ring distract you, and don't be self-conscious. Instead of thinking about how *you* look, pay attention to the judge and Primo at all times. If Primo is standing wrong or causing a disturbance, correct the situation immediately. Respond quickly to requests from the judge and other officials. Always be courteous and show good sportsmanship. Never crowd another exhibitor. Move smoothly, precisely yet naturally. Blend in nicely. Don't "upstage" Primo. (Meaning, don't draw attention to yourself that should go to him.)

Leading involves 0 to 15 points. The judge will post a pattern before the class. You'll enter the ring leading Primo at an alert walk, usually in a counterclockwise direction. Walk on Primo's left side and hold the lead shank in your right hand, near the halter. Carry the rest of the line neatly folded in your left hand. Follow the pattern and do whatever the judge asks. You'll lead Primo at a walk and trot, stop him, turn him to the right around his haunches, pose him and back him up as requested.

If you used ground work to teach Primo the in-gear and in-neutral verbal cues used in trails, he'll already move at your cluck and stop at your "Whoa."

Now he must lead in a mannerly way. You want him to move freely straight forward, at a walk or trot, with his head beside your shoulder. He shouldn't have to be pulled along. He should turn away from you by a nice turn on the haunches. He should back straight and stop when asked.

Squaring Up, or Setting Primo's Feet

Maybe Primo is trained for halter class. If he already squares up for line-up, don't overwork him on it now. Once he understands what's expected, he needs little practice.

However, even if Primo knows what he's supposed to do, you need to learn what you're supposed to do. You learned in Chapter 3 how to square him up from the saddle. Now we'll approach it from the ground. If Primo doesn't already know how to square up for halter, you can teach him how. Be very patient. Think like a horse. And use think-talk.

- Stand at Primo's near side and position his right hind foot first. Back him up or lead him forward until his right hind foot is straight and barely forward of the left hind foot. Then stop him to "set" his right foot.
- Next, work the left hind foot by putting pressure on the lead shank. Push back, then pull. Keep doing this until his left foot is square with the right. Then say "Whoa."

  If Primo's feet are too close together, you can teach him to move one by putting your foot next to his foot and gently tapping for him to move it. This system works for asking him to move the foot out, in, forward or back. You can use it for a show, as long as you don't kick his leg. (But then, you'd never do that.) However, *the best way to move Primo's hind or front feet in a show is to cue him with the lead line.* You can ask him to move his feet farther apart by turning his head. To move his left hind foot out a little wider, for example, turn his head to the right when you push or pull on the line. It "opens his door" like a rein cue.

If one of his hind feet is cocked up, you can do one of several things: (1) tap that hind foot with your toe, (2) tap the *front* foot on the *same* side with your toe, (3) bump him back by raising the lead shank or (4) grasp his tail at the base and gently push or pull it.

- For setting his front feet by tapping with your foot (mainly for schooling or halter class), also begin with the right side. Face Primo's tail and put your right hand on his withers as a brace. Touch his right foot with your right foot until he moves it where you want it. When he does, say "Whoa."

- Next, move to his left side and face his head. Brace with your right hand on his left shoulder and touch his left foot with your right foot until he moves it where you want it. Say "Whoa" when he has it in the right spot.

  It's best to follow the same order for setting Primo's feet. However, you can make some minor adjustments about which of your feet to use where, and whether to brace on his withers or shoulder. This depends on your size, Primo's size *and* what works best for your horse. Patiently "listen" to his signals. Learn his preferred way, then stay with it.

- After you have Primo squared up, move in front of him and face him. Stand about 18 inches from his head. Be where Primo is aware of you and you can watch the judge out of the corner of your eye. This lets Primo relax while he waits for the judge. It puts you close enough to keep him from moving his feet or hips. Don't bother him unless he acts restless or starts to move. Know your horse well enough to read his subtle body language. It's easier to stop a move *before* it happens than to get him back into position afterward. A mark of good horsemanship is for you to need only think-talk and perhaps slight finger motions to keep Primo quiet.

Posing and Showing Primo

When you see that the judge is about to look at Primo, move to the side opposite of where the judge is standing. This lets Primo see what's going on beyond you. He'll respond by raising his head and perking his ears up. Some of the other horses probably will get fidgety and sour from having to stand at attention. That's too bad. They didn't *have* to pose all that time. All Primo did was keep his feet still. Now he's alert and squared up, happy to pose for the judge. And if you're first in line, concentrate on setting Primo up. The judge will wait. Look at him when you're ready to show.

Look for subtle signals from the judge and obey them promptly. For example, when the judge is going down the lineup or having each entrant do a pattern, your turn may be signaled just by a look and a touch to the hat. This signals you to do what the others before you have done (or tried to do).

The Quarter Method

There are two reasons for using the quarter method. One is it keeps you from blocking the judge's view of Primo. The other, more important reason has to do with safety. Just in case Primo misbehaves, this method always keeps you in a good position to control him with the lead line. You can keep his hindquarters from swinging toward the judge and maybe kicking.

Imagine Primo divided into four sections, numbered clockwise, as in the drawing. You'll stay at the left or the right side of Primo's head while the judge moves all around him. Position yourself with the judge this way:

- When the judge is in #1, you are in #4 (left).
- When the judge moves to #2, you move to #1 (right).
- When the judge moves to #3, you return to #4.
- When the judge moves to #4, you move back to #1.

Keep showing until the entire class has been placed and everyone has been excused from the ring.

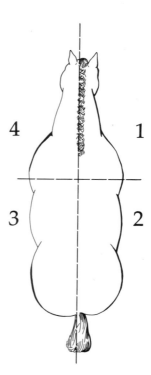

Quarter Method

APPENDIX 1

—◆◆◆—

FURTHER READING

General Information

The *Horse Industry Directory* is published by the American Horse Council, 1700 K Street, NW, Washington, DC 20006 (202-296-4031). A new directory comes out each year, with updated addresses of all organizations and registries and information about government sources, trade publications, equine health and educational data and the like. Price is $10.00.

The following books may be of interest to you.

Tack

The Howell Book of Saddlery and Tack by Elwyn Harley-Edwards (Howell Book House)
Filled with color photos and illustrations, this guide deals with equipment from around the world. It's a resource on topics ranging from the history of saddles to the use of training aids.

Tack Buyer's Guide by Charlene Strickland (Breakthrough Publications)
This handbook explains everything about the purchase and use of all kinds of tack: saddles, bridles, bits, blankets, barn equipment, specialty gear and much more. It tells how to recognize the good brands and gives money-saving tips that work.

Horse Care

Horse Owner's Veterinary Handbook by James M. Giffin, M.D. and Tom Gore, D.V.M. (Howell Book House)
This presents vital information in an easy-to-understand for-

mat, with a detailed table of contents. Special feature: an index of signs (for example: "muscle spasm," "peculiar stance") helps a reader determine what kind of problem his horse may have.

A–Z of Horse Diseases & Health Problems by Tim Hawcroft (Howell Book House)

This handbook by a veterinarian is arranged alphabetically, like a dictionary, and the color photos show you how to spot symptoms in their early stages so you can respond properly.

Show Grooming by Charlene Strickland (Breakthrough Publications)

This is a guide to outstanding show grooming.

Grooming to Win, 2nd ed, by Susan Harris (Howell Book House)

A guide for going from pasture to show ring, featuring both Western and English performance.

Western Horsemanship

Ride Western Style by Tommie Kirksmith (Howell Book House)

This is the first book available for boys and girls who want to learn Western riding. Obviously, I recommend it!

The Art of Western Riding by Bob Mayhew with John Birdsall (Howell Book House)

Bob Mayhew, who lives in England, wrote this to teach Western riding to Europeans, but it has sound information for anyone.

Think Harmony With Horses by Ray Hunt (Pioneer Publishing)

Ray Hunt revolutionized the Western way of schooling a horse by thinking harmony, as opposed to the rough, old methods of breaking a horse.

Western Training: Theory and Practice by Jack Brainard with Peter Phinny (Western Horseman)

This common-sense guide to Western training was written by a special horseman noted for his work with Quarter Horses.

Riding and Schooling the Western Performance Horse by G. F. Corley, D.V.M. (Prentice-Hall Press)

This excellent step-by-step instructional book explains the theories behind the mechanics of motion in order to understand what the horse is doing right or wrong.

Western Horsemanship by Richard Shrake (Western Horseman)
A very good guide to riding Western style.

Breaking and Showing the Cutting Horse by Lynn Champion (Breakthrough Publications)
This champion rider shares with readers her hands-on experience as well as advice from many top trainers and judges.

Cutting: A Guide for the Non-Pro Competitor by Sally Harrison (Howell Book House)
A very clear and complete guide to cutting, its history, great riders and horses, and techniques for winning.

Cutting by Leon Harrel (Western Horseman)
A paperback guide to cutting by a well-known horseman.

Reining by Bob Loomis with Cathy Kadash (Equimedia)
Explains the breeding and training methods Loomis used to become a world champion at reining nine times.

Reining: The Art of Performance in Horses by Al Dunning (Western Horseman)
A champion's complete guide to training/showing.

Running to Win by Martha Josey and Linda Clark (Josey Enterprise)
This is the definitive book on the art of running barrels.

Barrel Racing by Sharon Camarillo (Western Horseman)
Focuses on the selection of horse and equipment and the training and riding techniques necessary for winning.

Team Roping by Leo Camarillo (Western Horseman)
Covers all instructional aspects of this sport in words and pictures.

Long Distance Riding by Marcy Drummond (Howell Book House)
A book that will prepare you to enjoy what this sport has to offer.

If you can't find the books listed here at a bookstore or library, try one of the direct book marketers that specialize in horse books. They offer new books and reprints of horse books (including some classics) that are no longer available from the original publishing house or at regular bookstores. Places where you buy tack for Primo are also good sources.

Here are some direct marketers who offer free catalogs:

Breakthrough Publications, Inc., Millwood, NY 10546 (800-824-5000)

H. Kauffman & Sons Saddlery, 419 Park Avenue South, New York, NY 10016

Miller's Harness, 123 East 24th Street, New York, NY 10010

The Practice Ring, Inc., 7510 Allisonville Road, Indianapolis, IN 64250 (800-553-5319).

Schneider's Saddlery, 1609 Golden Gate Plaza, Cleveland, OH 44124 and 6245 East Bell Road, Scottsdale, AZ 85254 (1-800-365-1311 for a full-line horse catalog).

Videos

Videos can also be ordered from the direct marketers just listed, or you can contact these companies for instructional videos:

Farnam Companies, Inc., P.O. Box 12068, Omaha, NE 68112 (800-548-2828)

The Horseman's Source, Inc., 11435 Hungate, Colorado Springs, CO 80908 (800-325-1894)

Rodeo Video, Inc., P.O. Box G, Snowflake, AZ 85937 (602-536-7111).

Video Horse World, 205 W. Plymouth, Bremen, IN 46506 (800-445-0833).

Roping Schools and Clinics*

Butch Meyer's Clinics, Rt. 6, Box 6455, Athens, TX 75751 (214-675-1532)

*Thanks to Fred Westergaard's article "Ropers: Take Aim on Training!" in the July 1990 issue of *Horse and Rider*.

Jake Barnes and Clay O'Brien Cooper Team Roping School, c/o Fred or Chris Wahl, 9440 Lake Road, Wisconsin Rapids, WI 54494 (715-424-4561)

Calf Roping Clinic, Gary Johnson, Schutter, OK 74460, (918-652-8357 days, 918-652-3033 nights)

Guy Allen Steer Roping School, Steve Harmon, Box 1360, Beaver, OK 73932 (405-625-3051 or 405-625-4564)

World Champion Rodeo Schools, 555 E. McDowell, Mesa, AZ 85203 (602-464-0090)

Josey Enterprises, Inc., Route 2, Box 235, Karnack, TX 75661 (214-935-9279 or 214-935-5358)

APPENDIX 2

AHSA Equitation Seat Chart*

	Good	Minor Faults	Major Faults	Elimination
SEAT	keeping center of balance complete contact with saddle straight back	sitting off center sway back round back losing center of balance	excessive body motion popping out of saddle	falling off horse (refer to Art. 3713)

	Good	Minor Faults	Major Faults	Elimination
HANDS	quiet light hands maintaining consistent head position proper position (diagrams on pages 202 and 203 in the *AHSA Rule Book*)	unsteadiness incorrect position	horse's mouth gapping heavy hands constant bumping restrictions causing untrue gaits touching horse less than	two handing reins finger between romal reins more than one finger between split reins

	Good	*Minor Faults*	*Major Faults*	*Elimination*
			16″ of rein slack between hands touching saddle to prevent fall	

	Good	*Minor Faults*	*Major Faults*	*Elimination*
LEGS	secure leg position proper weight in stirrups controlling motion weight evenly on ball of foot heels lower than toes	uneven stirrups motion in legs insufficient weight in stirrups incorrect position	excess spurring loss of contact between legs & saddle/ foot & stirrups loss of stirrup	touching in front of cinch

	Good	*Minor Faults*	*Major Faults*	*Elimination*
CONTROL	maintaining horse in good form at consistent gaits ability to maintain horse under adverse conditions	breaking from walk to jog breaking from jog to lope not standing in line up	breaking from jog to walk breaking from lope to jog allowing horse to back crooked missing leads failure to back	[none]

	Good	*Minor Faults*	*Major Faults*	*Elimination*
OVERALL APPEAR- ANCE	suitable well-fitted outfit well-groomed horse clean equipment	saddle not suitable to rider's size unfitted outfit dirty boots ungroomed horse uncleaned equipment	improper appointments	illegal equipment

	Good	*Minor Faults*	*Major Faults*	*Elimination*
GENERAL	good attitude toward horse and judge consistency of rider's form	equipment not fitting horse failure to use corners and rail suitability of horse and rider	excessive voice commands excessive circling major delays in transitions	schooling horse off pattern

APPENDIX 3

---◄◄●►►---

Associations for Young Western Performance Riders

While this list offers a wide variety, it does not include every association involved with youth stock-seat competition. If Primo is breed-registered, contact the national registry for a local club. For help with finding an address, try the American Horse Council, 1700 K Street NW, Suite 300, Washington, DC 20006 (202-296-4031).

- The American Endurance Ride Conference does not have a separate youth division, but it does award the highest scoring youth in a competition. Ride and Tie Association recognizes the youngest winning team. Contact AERC at 701 High Street, #203, Auburn, CA 95603 (916-823-2260); or Ride and Tie, 1865 Indian Valley Road, Novato, CA 94947 (415-897-1829).
- The American Horse Shows Association has a stock seat medal class for junior members (under eighteen) of the AHSA. Contact AHSA Stock Seat Equitation Committee, 220 East 42nd Street, #409, New York, NY 10017-5806 (212-972-2472).
- The American Junior Rodeo Association, Box 481, Rankin, TX 79778 (no phone) oversees many rodeo events for youth.
- The American Paint Horse Association has a program for junior (eighteen and under) competition (AJPHA). They also have an Outside Competitive Activities program that gives credit and recognition for members who participate in approved shows and activities outside of APHA. Contact AJPHA at P.O. Box 961023, Fort Worth, TX 76161 (817-439-3400).

- The American Quarter Horse Association gives recognition for outstanding achievements in special events outside of AQHA. In addition, they have two programs for young members. Their junior division (AJQHA) focuses on young riders interested in competition. The other program has a reward-type plan for riding a Quarter Horse. After riding 50 hours, for example, you get a patch. Contact AJQHA or the AQHA Horseback Riding Program at P.O. Box 200, Amarillo, TX 79168 (806-376-4811).
- The Appaloosa Horse Club has a good youth program and network of regional clubs. Contact ApHC, Inc., P.O. Box 8403, Moscow, ID 83843 (208-882-5578).
- The International Arabian Horse Association includes Arabians, Half-Arabians and Anglo-Arabians. For information on youth stock-seat activities, contact IAHA at P.O. Box 33696, Denver, CO 80233 (303-450-4774).
- The Tennessee Walking Horse Breeders & Exhibitors Association has the following Western competitions: Western Pleasure, Reining, Trail, Poles and Barrels, Western Riding, Good Seat and Hands (Western or English). Contact TWHBEA at P.O. Box 286, Lewisburg, TN 37091 (615-359-1574).
- Josey Enterprises, Inc. (Route 2, Box 235, Karnack, TX 75661, 903-935-5358) has complete information on barrel racing and calf roping, including a list of clubs.
- The National Cutting Horse Association is one example of a breed-approved "outside activity." (Paint and Quarter Horse programs accredit / recognize members who earn laurels at activities other than these offered at Paint or Quarter Horse shows.) For information on their Youth Division (eighteen and under), contact NCHA, 4704 Highway 377 South, Fort Worth, TX 76116-8805 (817-244-6188).
- The National 4-H Council is a youth program for those nine through nineteen. Their shows (open to all registered

breeds *and* grade horses) include all the usual Western classes plus precision and drill teams. Look under Cooperative Extension Service in your local telephone directory under county or governmental agency listings. Ask if they have a local 4-H horse program or club. If not, contact National 4-H Supply Service, 7100 Connecticut Avenue, Chevy Chase, MD 20815 (301-961-2945).

- The National Reining Horse Association is another example of AQHA/APHA-approved "outside activity." For information about their Youth Division, contact NRHA, 28881 SR 83, Coshocton, OH 43812 (614-622-5611).
- The National Little Britches Rodeo is for riders between the ages of eight and eighteen. For information contact NLBR, 1045 W. Rio Grande, Colorado Springs, CO 80906 (303-389-0333).
- The National High School Rodeo Association is for riders in grades 9 through 12. Contact NHSRA, 12200 Pecos, #120, Denver, CO 80234 (303-452-0820).

INDEX

above the bit, defined, 30
aids
  artificial, 39–40
  natural, 34–37
American Buckskin Horse
  Association (ABHA),
  49–50
American Horse Shows
  Association (AHSA), 50,
  83, 84, 145
American Morgan Horse
  Association (AMHA), 49
American Paint Horse
  Association (APHA), 26,
  28, 49, 84, 145, 193
American Quarter Horse, 1
American Quarter Horse
  Association (AQHA), 26,
  27, 28, 49, 61, 84, 145, 193
anatomy
  horse's, 12–19, *illustrations
  14, 16, 17*
  rider's, 30–34, *illustration 31*
Appaloosa Horse Club
  (ApHC), 49
Appaloosas, 1
appointments, 80–85
Arabians, 1, 148–149
arena, 8

backing, 95–97,162,
  illustrations 125–127
  as discipline, *illustration 187*
bad habits, 72–74
bailing out, 42–43, *illustrations
  43–45*
bailing out (falling), 42–43

balance
  center of, 15–17
  in motion, 12–13
  static, 12
  two-point, 62–63
bareback riding, 74
barrel racing, 213; *illustrations
  231–233*
behind the bit, defined, 30
Bennett, Dr. Deb, 13
bit, 30, 51, 84
body movements, and control,
  39–40
boots, 39–40, 82
breathing, 33
build, rider's, 30–34
bumping, 75

calf roping, 197, *illustrations
  204–209*
  breakaway, 201, *illustration
  204*
  dally team, 201–202
camcorder, 8
canter, 22, 23, 24, 25, 28
  countercanter, 25, 165–167,
  illustration 170
  cross-canter, 25
center of balance (CB), 15–17
chaps, 39, 81–82
cinch, 97
circling, 151–154
class event, 50
class routine, 144–145
clothes, 80–83
coach, 7, 56
competitive trail riding, 4